WEET

by

John Wilson

Illustrated by Janice Armstrong

Napoleon Publishing

Published by Napoleon Publishing
Toronto Ontario Canada

Napoleon Publishing gratefully acknowledges
the support of The Canada Council.

Cover illustration by Steve Pilcher
Cover design by Donna Gedeon
Book design by Pamela Kinney

Canadian Cataloguing in Publication Data

Wilson, John (John Alexander), 1951-
Weet

ISBN 0-929141-40-7

I. Armstrong, Janice, 1953- . II. Title.

PS8595.I57W44 1995 jC813'.54 C95-931599-3
PZ7.W55We 1995

Printed and bound in Canada

Dedication:

For Sarah, Iain and Fiona, the original Weet

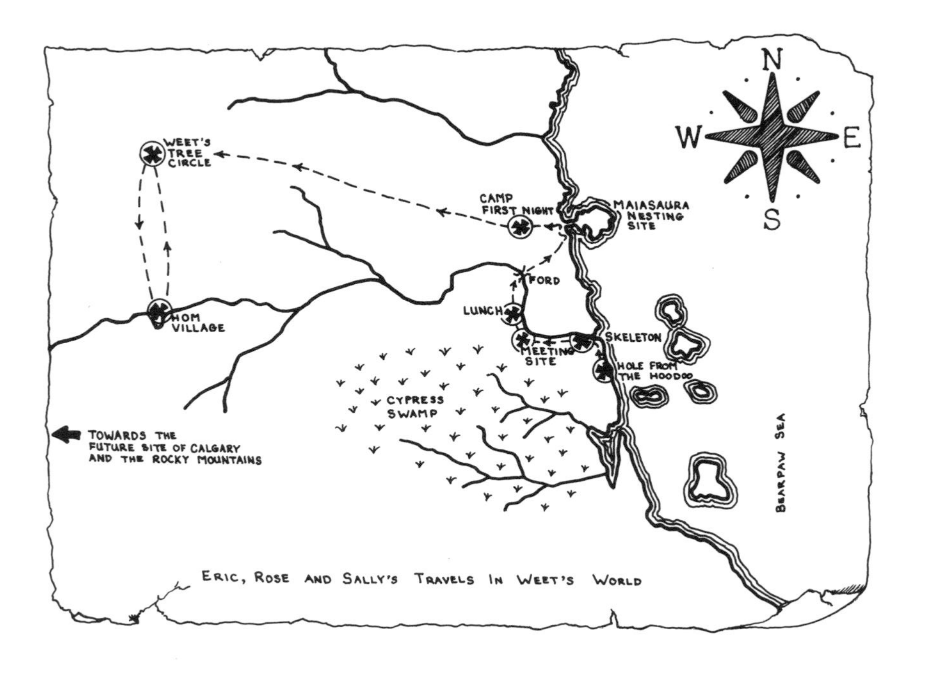
N
W
E
S
WEET'S TREE CIRCLE
CAMP FIRST NIGHT
MAIASAURA NESTING SITE
FORD
LUNCH
HOM VILLAGE
SKELETON
MEETING SITE
HOLE FROM THE HOODOO
CYPRESS SWAMP
TOWARDS THE FUTURE SITE OF CALGARY AND THE ROCKY MOUNTAINS
BEARPAW SEA
ERIC, ROSE AND SALLY'S TRAVELS IN WEET'S WORLD

CHAPTER 1

Saved by Mathematics

It was the first time Eric had ever understood the true meaning of the expression 'rooted to the spot.' Like so many of the things adults said, it hadn't seemed to make any sense before. Now it did. His toes had become long, gnarled roots, anchored deep in the earth below him. He could feel them pushing their way through the soil and into the cracks in the rock beneath. They were reaching past the fossilized remains of ancient worlds, down to the hot, molten core of the planet itself.

The legs on top of this remarkable root system were also rapidly becoming wooden. A numbness was creeping up towards his thighs. He felt sure that if he looked down his legs would be covered with peeling bark and his knees would be two ugly knots of wood. But he couldn't look down. The creature in front of him commanded his total attention. What's more, it was approaching at a fearsome speed.

The beast stood no more than four feet high, although its length was almost twice that. It ran on two powerful hind legs with its graceful head thrust forward. The head was balanced at the other end by a long, rigid tail. Two aspects of the animal's appearance were particularly important to Eric. The first was its oversized, curved teeth. They were arranged in a mouth which, he felt uncomfortably certain, could surround his head with ease. The second was the six-inch-long, dagger-like claw attached to one of the toes on each hind foot. The creature had to keep the claws raised to prevent itself from tripping. As the forelegs reached out eagerly to grasp him, Eric could imagine what those dreadful claws were about to do.

It seemed terribly unfair to Eric that this messy end should occur only three days before his twelfth birthday. What would his parents do with the new baseball glove and video game which lay, neatly wrapped, in the bottom of the closet? On the other hand, he was glad he had decided against doing Monday's math homework. Adding up numbers seemed a particularly pointless way to spend your last hours.

The velociraptor (Eric was fairly sure that was what it was) was almost upon him now. Eric could clearly see the pupils of its red eyes and the rough scaly texture of its greenish skin. Its breath was warm and foul on his face. He closed his eyes.

Nothing happened. At least, nothing happened to Eric, except that he felt a rush of air as the velociraptor sped past. When he opened his eyes, it was gone.

A scream over his left shoulder made him turn

around, just in time to see a green back disappearing into the undergrowth. Mr. Smith, his math teacher, was clutched helplessly in the beast's forefeet. His screams for help were mixed with shouted promises of impossibly good grades if Eric would come to his rescue.

The offer was certainly tempting, but Eric had no choice in the matter. His toes had almost reached China and his legs had become completely numb. In addition, there was an irritating buzzing noise beside his head.

As the dream faded and he drifted back to wakefulness, the first question in Eric's befuddled mind was why the alarm was going off on a Sunday. The second, as he tried to roll over to switch it off, was why his legs were still numb. An experimental kick merely produced a grunt from the thirty pounds of brown hair lying across his knees.

"Sally, get off or I'll kick you off."

Within the shapeless mass of brown, a crescent of white appeared as an eye opened and attempted to gauge the seriousness of the threat. Apparently unconvinced of any danger, the eye closed again.

"Sally!" By rolling onto his side and drawing his legs up, Eric was able to pull them from underneath the dog. As he straightened them again, Sally and the bedclothes were pushed in a tangled heap to the foot of the bed. With a lot of grumbling, Sally edged over the bed onto the floor, where she began a complex routine of stretches and yawns.

CHAPTER 2

Breakfast Conversations

Eric switched off the alarm. It was already fully light and noises were coming from the kitchen downstairs. Drumheller, badlands, dinosaur bones — that explained everything — why he had dreamt about dinosaurs, why the alarm was set, and why he had decided to ignore his math assignment. It was late in October, possibly the last good weekend before winter, and his parents had agreed to spend the day in the badlands of southern Alberta.

Mr. and Mrs. Richardson lived in Calgary. The fact that this was a day stolen from winter was the only thing that made this trip to Drumheller remarkable. There were two main reasons why the Richardson family went east to the prairies for a day out rather than west into the Rocky Mountains. The first was that everyone else went to the mountains and the accessible areas tended to be crowded. The other was their son's fanatical interest in dinosaurs.

Ever since he could remember, Eric had been fascinated by these huge monsters which had roamed the earth so near his home. His active imagination recreated their world and puzzled over their mysterious disappearance. His bedroom was covered with pictures of dinosaurs, and his bookcase was filled with books about them. He even had a collection of fossilized bones in a box under his bed. At every opportunity, he put as much pressure as possible on his parents to drive out to the country to let him rummage around in the steep, narrow valleys for fragments of this lost world.

An added bonus from Eric's point of view was that the dry world of the badlands didn't irritate his impressive collection of allergies. Anywhere else, there was a very real danger that he would stumble onto some flower or other that would start his nose running and set him sneezing uncontrollably.

Apart from the fact that everyone was glad to be free of his sneezing fits, the rest of the family didn't share Eric's enthusiasm for the badlands. Sally did enjoy accompanying him on these excursions, but her main interest was in bones of a more recent vintage than the ones he was searching for. To be fair to his parents, they tried to express an interest in his treasures, but they didn't seem to have his talent for conjuring up vivid pictures of the long-dead owners from the fragments of tooth or bone. They seemed much happier just sitting reading in the sun or going off on walks.

When they went off on their own, (usually only to the limit of hearing), they left Eric in charge of his just-turned-seven-year-old sister, Rose. Unfortunately, Rose was the family member least interested in his hobby. To her, crawling around on one's hands and knees looking at the ground was silly and childish, and she never tired of telling Eric this. However, the passion that drove him was so strong that he accepted having to drag Rose around as a fair price to pay.

At first, Eric had attempted to share his excitement when he uncovered a piece of tooth or a turtle scale. Once he had almost caught a glimmer of interest as he proudly announced the discovery of half a triceratops toe. But when Rose had found out that triceratops had toes that looked nothing like her own (and in any case were made out of boring stone), her flicker of interest had died and she had gone back to complaining about the heat and dust. Eric had given up trying to make a convert out of his sister.

To Sally's surprise, Eric leapt out of bed, threw on his clothes with unaccustomed haste and disappeared out of the room. In a flash, he was back rummaging in a drawer for his combination knife, saw, compass, fishing line and matches. This meant that today was certainly not a school day, Sally thought, despite the noisy thing beside the bed. Perhaps it meant an excursion? Wagging her tail hopefully, she trotted out the door after him.

Half-way down the stairs, Eric overheard his parents' breakfast conversation. It was a topic which interested him, so he stopped to listen.

"If this study is right," his father was saying, "it means that the climate could be warming up faster than anyone expected."

Peering through the banisters, Eric could see his father with the paper open on the table in front of him.

"But it's only one study, and there's so much uncertainty in the results." As usual, his mother was taking the most positive approach.

"Yes," agreed his father, "but we can see things changing around us. Look outside – it's the end of October and it's like a summer's day. And this is no longer unusual. In the last few years, it seems winter hasn't started until Christmas, and it's over by February. It's nice that we can get out of town this late in the year, but it's difficult for the farmers if there's not enough winter snow. And don't forget, if the sea level does begin to rise, your mother in Vancouver will have trouble."

The changing weather was a common topic around the house these days. The way his parents discussed it worried Eric because, when they thought he wasn't listening, they sounded unhappy. However, when he thought about it, it didn't seem too bad. Of course, if Vancouver did sink beneath the Pacific, it would mean that they wouldn't be able to go and visit Gran out on the coast any more, but perhaps she would come and live with them. That would more than make up for not going to the beach, because Gran's stories were the real reason that he looked forward to their visits. She had lived her early life in exotic places like India and Africa and had an endless supply of stories, some of which may even have been true. If she came to stay, it would mean a lot more stories.

Worrying about the farmers not growing enough food didn't really seem worthwhile to him either.

When the problem with the farmers had first been overheard, Eric had discussed it with Rose. She had not been worried, but with her usual direct approach had asked the man who sold hot dogs at the small baseball ground around the corner how many he had left. The man had laughed and said, "A million million."

Eric and Rose had had a good laugh wondering if there were a computer somewhere that kept track of hot dogs, and how long a million million would last shared among the sixty or seventy people who went to each game. Even if the figure were only a rough estimate, there would be hot dogs enough for quite a long time. One of the few things Eric and Rose agreed on was that almost all food other than hot dogs was unnecessary and was only forced on kids because their parents had been forced to eat it when they were growing up.

As far as Eric could see, the changes in the weather were only bringing advantages. This final, sunny Sunday afternoon before he became old was one of them.

The real reason for Eric's interest in his parents' conversations was that he knew that changes in the weather may have been at least one of the reasons why dinosaurs had died out. Since the discovery of the huge Chicxulub crater in Mexico, few people doubted that a meteorite or comet had put an end to the dinosaurs' rule.

But they hadn't all been killed by the impact, or the shockwave, or even the continent-wide fires that followed. What had finished them off had been the months of total, impenetrable darkness caused by all the material thrown up into the upper atmosphere. That cold, unnatural night would have killed off the plants on which the browsing animals depended, even if it had not killed them directly.

As the plant-eaters disappeared, the meat-eaters, even the smaller ones, starved. Only the tiny burrowing mammals, that were used to the dark and did not rely on plants for food, survived to become the great-great-grandfathers of one of the most dramatic comebacks in the history of life.

There was even some evidence to suggest that the climate had been changing before that long ago meteorite arrived. For several million years, the numbers of dinosaur species seemed to have been declining. Some people suggested that a series of smaller meteorites had been crashing into the earth and gradually altering the balmy Cretaceous weather before the 'big one' hit. Unfortunately, no one seemed able to decide whether the climate had become too wet or too dry or too hot or too cold.

Whatever the case, weather had been important to the last of the dinosaurs, and it was becoming important to Eric. This connection with the dinosaurs' world brought Eric closer to their lost time. His main hope was that a meteorite wouldn't make their worlds too similar.

The conversation downstairs was interrupted by Rose demanding more toast and Sally pleading to be let out, so Eric continued on down.

Sunday breakfasts were always long-drawn-out, but this one was interminable. Finally, it was over, lunch was packed and everyone was organized and seated in the car. They were heading east to the land of the dinosaurs.

CHAPTER 3

An End

As Eric watched the brown prairies roll past the car window, he let his imagination drift back in time. In his mind, the landscape turned green and lush. The road began to glisten and became a wide, sluggish river winding east to the broad, shallow Bearpaw Sea. Behind him, the towering Rocky Mountains shrank into a shadow of their future selves. Sixty-five million years slipped by in a minute. The tropical vegetation of the Cretaceous hid all manner of wonders from Eric's too-eager eyes. He was just imagining a rustle in the foliage which might turn into a life-and-death struggle between a horned triceratops and a hungry tyrannosaurus, when a sharp pain in his ribs interrupted his reverie.

"Come on, wake up, we're there." Rose poked him again, even harder. "It was you who wanted to come. Don't go to sleep."

"I wasn't asleep. I was thinking."

"About big lizards eating cities, I suppose." Rose sounded petulant. "King Kong didn't live here anyway. He lived in Africa."

"King Kong wasn't a lizard. You're thinking of Godzilla. Anyway, when the dinosaurs were here this place probably looked a lot more like Africa than it does now." Rose knew all this – Eric had told her a hundred times. She was just trying to annoy him. It was going to be a difficult day.

"Mom, Eric's imagining things."

"Stop bickering you two. We'll be out of the car in a minute." Their father sounded tired.

The car turned into a small parking lot beside the road. It was Eric's favourite spot. The valley was wide here and, in the middle, a sluggish, muddy river meandered sleepily among some willows. Opposite, the valley edge stretched away in both directions, defining the limits of a catastrophic flood which had swept down from some long-vanished glacial lake.

Yet it was not the view that held Eric's attention. Much closer, on the other side of the road, the land sloped up in a jumbled mass of weird, carved shapes. Known locally as hoodoos, they were the results of rain and wind carving into the soft sandstones of the cliff. Some were simple rounded lumps, but others soared upward to end in slender pinnacles topped by caps of harder rock. It would have been easy to become completely lost among them, had it not been for the fact that the ground on which they sat sloped gently down to the road. If you became lost, all you had to do was to keep going downhill to reach the highway.

Eric searched for his fossils on the ground between the hoodoos. Harder than the surrounding rock, bone fragments tended to weather out and collect at the base of the slopes. Sometimes he would look at the hoodoos themselves hoping to discover bones still in place. They were more difficult to spot, but they might be the tip of a skull, or even a complete skeleton. Then the find might be excavated and displayed by the museum, and Eric would have his name on a plaque beside it. Sometimes, when he was feeling generous, he would imagine Sally's and even Rose's name on the plaque beside his, but mostly he was alone in his fame.

Not that Eric craved fame. It would be nice, but mainly it would allow him to pursue his dream of becoming a 'bone detective.' Then he would be able to go where he wanted: to Utah, where the vast sauropods had lived, to Europe, where the very first dinosaurs had been uncovered over a century-and-a-half ago, and to the Gobi desert, where American paleontologist Roy Chapman Andrews had carried his pearl-handled Colt 45 to the first dinosaur nests, like some real-life Indiana Jones.

Fame would be nice all right. Eric twirled an imaginary revolver around his finger and set off across the deserted road.

Eric's parents found a quiet, sheltered spot to lay out the bulky possessions necessary for any family outing. Eric was hardly a part of the family, so strong was the urge that pulled him away to search the ground on the small tributary valley running up towards the cliffs. Sally was already busy with her canine explorations.

"Don't go too far, and keep an eye on Rose," his mother was shouting after him. "We'll have lunch in about an hour."

Eric didn't go far, just behind a couple of hoodoos. As long as he was out of sight, he found that his parents' world was easily forgotten. Rose didn't require much looking after. As soon as Eric stopped, she settled down to draw pictures in the soft ground. Sally rushed around, apparently aimlessly, sniffing in corners and scratching under stones.

It was already getting quite hot in this little valley and Eric had to stop his searching a couple of times to answer Rose's request for water. The first hour or so, before Rose got bored, was usually the most productive. This morning, however, Eric's diligent searching had only produced a few odd fragments, hardly worth the bother of taking home.

"Sally's gone in a hole!" Rose shouted from a narrow cleft between two hoodoos.

"She's probably just hot and has gone to lie down." Eric had noticed on previous occasions that being covered with brown hair was not an advantage in these hot valleys. Sally often found dark, shaded corners or holes to rest in.

"No, she's gone right in." Rose was beginning to sound worried.

Grumbling, Eric wandered across to see what the problem was. Rose was standing in front of a small hole in the wall of a hoodoo. It was round and about two feet high. He crouched down and peered in. It was pitch black and quite cold. He called Sally's name a few times without any response. Eric withdrew his head. There was a flashlight in the car. He had only taken one step to go back and get it when someone took a photograph.

At least, that was his first impression: someone with a giant camera had suddenly taken a flash photograph of the world. But the weird, bright light didn't go out. Instinctively, Eric looked up. Before him was a scene that he had imagined a hundred times. The light was coming from a huge ball of fire which was tearing across the sky, trailing flame and steam behind it. He knew it was a meteorite, but how big was it? Was it small and close by or the size of a mountain and far away? Was this the last thing the dinosaurs had seen? He shivered in the warm air. Maybe this was the last thing he would see.

CHAPTER 4

A Beginning

Rose's scream brought his attention back. Grabbing her by the waist, he pushed her into the dark hole in the rock and crawled in after. If it was the end of the world, the hole wouldn't do him much good, but, despite the dark and the cold, he felt safer.

Rose's scream had died away to choking sobs and whimpers. The small cave seemed to be a tunnel. The further they went, the safer they would be. Sally must be ahead somewhere. Pushing Rose in front of him, Eric edged along in the dark.

"I want to go home, I'm scared." Rose's fear had turned to a vocal stage. "Mommy will be cross at you for pushing me in here. If we get lost, no one will ever find us."

"It's all right, we'll just find Sally and go back for lunch. We can't get lost in a tunnel." With a combination of persuasion and shoves, Eric moved Rose slowly through the blackness. In any case, talking made him feel better, in the same way that when he was younger, he talked to the monsters under his bed to make them go away.

The tunnel curved around to the left. It was like those curves on the highway which seem to go on so long that you must surely arrive back where you started. He continued talking and pushing. His head was right behind Rose and all he could see were the backs of her legs in dirty white trousers. It was silly to wear white on a day like this, but they were Rose's favourites.

He could see Rose's trousers! Raising his head to look over her shoulder, he could see a patch of light ahead. They must have crawled completely through the hoodoo. The light was hazy, almost as if a lace curtain covered the entrance.

"Look, there's the end of the tunnel. Sally's probably waiting for us and we can go and have lunch." Rose speeded up noticeably at this thought.

The light gradually increased until Eric had no trouble seeing the walls on either side. The tunnel mouth was not bright because it was covered by a mat of hanging vegetation. This was strange. Vegetation in the badlands usually only consisted of a few hardy cacti. Untroubled by such concerns, Rose pushed her way through and disappeared with a startled shout.

More cautiously, Eric pushed his head through the foliage. The tunnel ended in a hole similar to the one they had entered. However, this one was about six feet above the ground. The floor was black mud which oozed between Eric's fingers and sucked at his knees. A surprised Rose was sitting at the bottom of the slope. She was covered in mud and bits of leaf were stuck to her hair.

"Where are we?" she wailed. "Where are Mommy and Daddy? I'm all muddy."

"It's all right," shouted Eric, with a confidence he didn't entirely feel. "I'll help you up and then we'll go and find them." Unsure of how he was going to fulfill his promise, he looked at their surroundings.

The view he saw took his breath away. Rose sat on the edge of a wide, flat mudplain which stretched away in all directions. In the distance, the black mud was cut by a silver streak which could only be a large lake or sea. Closer in, islands rose out of the mud. They were not large, but managed to support lush vegetation. Several different kinds of trees were growing there amid an underbrush of assorted bushes and shrubs. The whole scene was bathed in a diffuse light, as if the sun were shining through high clouds. It all looked very strange, yet vaguely familiar.

The sense of familiarity made Eric assume that the shadow he saw was that of a small plane. It was skimming across the mud flats, roughly parallel to the bank out of which he was peering. Expecting to see a Cessna, he looked up. It was the right size for a Cessna, but no plane Eric knew of was covered in fur and flapped its wings. The creature was flying at tree-top height and was turning its head from side-to-side. The enormous, slowly-flapping wings were a pale grey underneath and almost black on top. The black head was balanced on an s-shaped neck. The head consisted of two parts separated by a vivid streak of white which swept back from the large eye. The back of the head

stretched out into a long, aerodynamic crest, half as long as Eric was tall. Its obvious purpose was to balance the other half, which consisted almost entirely of long, pointed jaws lined with dozens of needle-sharp teeth. As it drew level with Eric, the creature swivelled its head and fixed him with a cold, hungry stare.

Eric's first reaction was to retreat into the tunnel, but his weight put too much of a strain on the weak mud of the bank. In an avalanche of wet mud and branches, he crashed down the slope to join his sister. His first thought at the bottom was to see if the creature still considered him a possible snack. Apparently it did not. It had banked away and was soaring out over the offshore islands.

"Watch out, you almost buried me!" Rose's moods could swing from one extreme to the other. One minute she was terrified, the next angry. Any second now, she might burst out laughing.

Her brother didn't feel much like laughing.

Struggling out of the mass of clinging mud which he had dislodged, he looked back up. The hole they had crawled out of was gone. It must have been close to the top of the bank, but a large section had collapsed and hidden it. All attempts to climb the bank only brought more foul mud down on top of them.

Eric sat down dejectedly. Rose began to sob again. "I told you we would get lost in that silly tunnel. How are we ever going to get home? It's lunch-time and I'm hungry."

"I don't know." Eric's reply was to more than his sister's question. His head was filled with ideas he could hardly put into words. He was pretty sure that he had seen a pteranodon, a creature that had populated the skies above the dinosaurs and had died out with them, sixty-five million years before Eric and Rose were born. How had they got where they were, wherever and whenever that was? How were they going to survive now that they were here? What had happened to their own world? How could they ever get back to it?

Eric envied his sister. The impossibility of their apparent arrival in a different world didn't worry her. An empty stomach could take precedence over almost anything. Not being able to think of anything better to do, Eric reached down and pinched himself hard. It hurt all right, but was it possible to dream that you had pinched yourself? He leaned over and pinched Rose.

"Ow! What did you do that for?"

"Sorry, I was just seeing if you were dreaming."

"Of course, I'm not dreaming." Rose had swung back to being angry. "I don't dream about flying dragons and muddy swamps. This is your stupid dream."

A rustling in the undergrowth above their heads made them both look up. Visions of fearsome claws and teeth flashed through Eric's mind, but what he did see made him laugh despite himself. Peering through the green at the top of the bank was a familiar brown face. The hair was wet and matted and, somewhere behind the face, an invisible tail was happily rustling the bushes. Not all the joy was due to their reunion, for, clenched firmly between the teeth, was a bone worthy of any canine hall of fame.

"Come on, Sally old girl! Come on down and join us."

The dog attempted a dignified entrance, but the weight of the bone and the slippery mud combined to deposit her in a messy heap at the bottom of the slope. She was immediately set upon by both of the children, and all three and the bone rolled around happily in the mud.

"Well," said Eric, as they settled down, "at least we have the only dog in the world who has chewed on a dinosaur bone. If this really is the Cretaceous, we're probably the largest mammals on the earth."

Sally cocked her head, as if she didn't find that information particularly comforting.

"Anyhow, there must be a way up the bank if Sally got up there. There doesn't seem to be any point in staying here, so let's start exploring."

Sally's footprints in the mud were easy to find, and the three of them began following them along the bottom of the bank. As they squelched along in stunned silence, Eric began to notice details of their surroundings. The air was humid and heavy, rather like the summer they had gone to Disneyland. Yet there seemed to be an underlying, damp chill in the air. The vegetation overhanging the bank looked almost tropical, with broad oval leaves and scattered bright orange and red flowers, but some of the trees looked like oaks or even firs and pines. Insects buzzed around the flowers and the occasional, familiar mosquito hummed past Eric's head. These were the only sounds.

Eric squashed quite a few annoying bugs before he suddenly remembered a story he had once read and stopped with a worried look on his face. The tale had been about time travel and groups of people who had paid large sums of money to go into the past of their choice. All the travellers were warned not to alter anything because of the unforeseen effect it might have on the present. He couldn't remember the details, but, in the end, the present had been drastically changed because of a long, complex string of events which had started with someone thoughtlessly stepping on a beetle.

An uncomfortable picture swam into his mind. In it, Calgary, his parents and his world slowly faded away into nothingness, because the last mosquito he had killed had been destined to be supper for the small rodent from which he was evolved. He made a mental note to try and disturb things as little as possible, just in case they did manage to get back into his present.

After a few minutes walking, they were faced with a wide, shallow river. As soon as she saw it, Sally bounded forward to splash happily in the water. Eric went over and experimentally put in a hand.

"It's warm," he said. "At least we can have a wash."

They all felt better after cleaning off some of the clinging black slime, although their clothes and hair would take a while to dry in the damp air. The activity also brought back Rose's voice.

"Where are we, Eric?" she asked mournfully.

"I think a better question would be: when are we?" replied her brother, as he sat wringing out one of his socks. "I think we came out of the hole in the same place we went in. The problem is that, somehow, we've travelled in time."

"But that's impossible," interrupted Rose. "Time travel only happens in stories."

"I know," said Eric, "but I don't see how else we can explain all this. Maybe that hole was a time warp or maybe the meteorite did something to time. I don't know, but it looks like we've jumped in time. That flying thing was a pteranodon."

"A dinosaur?" asked Rose.

"Probably not," Eric replied. "Pteranodons weren't dinosaurs. They were pterosaurs, but they did live at the same time. If any of this makes sense, we should be in the time when the rocks we crawled through were laid down. That would put us right at the end of the Cretaceous Period, about 65 million years ago."

"What are we going to do?" asked Rose miserably. Even when she was in their world, Rose wasn't particularly interested in things with long names. "How are we going to get home?"

Eric didn't have the faintest idea.

"There must be a way back," he said in a voice he hoped sounded reassuring. "After all, there was a way here."

Before his brain had time to come up with any more concrete answers, Sally finished her wash, shook herself vigorously and set off upstream.

"I guess that's the way we should go," said Eric, grasping at straws. "At least, the ground looks firmer and we can always get back by following the river."

He could not imagine why they would want to

return. He didn't tell Rose, but he was beginning to think they were stuck here. If that were the case, one place was as good as another. However, activity seemed to make Rose feel better, so they set off after the dog.

CHAPTER 5

Weet

Once they turned inland, the going was much more comfortable, the ground was harder and the trees were a bit more spread out. Even the underbrush grew in clumps which were easy to walk around.

As they turned a corner in the river, they discovered the reason for Sally's hurried departure. Half-buried in the sand of the river bank was a huge skull. It was lying on its side with one empty eye socket staring up at the sky. Behind it were scattered rib and leg bones, in the middle of which lay a contented dog. Eric guessed that, from the strange crest on top of the skull, Sally had found the remains of a plant-eating hadrosaur which had fallen in and drowned when the river was last in flood. That would make it the end of the Cretaceous for sure.

"So that's where you got your bone," he said. "Well, come on, find a small one and let's see what else we can find."

The dog picked up a small rib and, with only a short sorrowful look back at her idea of heaven, followed them through the trees.

As they walked along, Sally became more adventurous and roamed further and further afield. Rose was too overwhelmed to complain about her hunger, although she was beginning to glance longingly at some round, brownish fruit on the bushes they passed. Eric was musing on how inaccurate the paintings of the dinosaurs' world were in the books he had read. They always depicted frantic activity, whereas in reality, (if this was reality), all they had seen was a solitary, soaring pteranodon and a very inactive skeleton. This place seemed almost empty.

He was proved rudely wrong by Sally's sudden appearance through a clump of small trees. She had lost her hadrosaur rib and was running flat out as if her life depended on it. It probably did. A crashing in the undergrowth drew his attention to a sight that was all too frighteningly familiar to Eric. Complete with razor-sharp teeth and claw, the velociraptor burst into the clearing. Unlike the one in Eric's dream, it was covered in black and yellow feathers and had an orange, beak-like mouth, but those were details for scientists of the future to argue about. This one took one look at Eric, with Rose and Sally cowering behind him, saw lunch and headed in their direction.

The feeling of having been there before didn't extend to Eric's legs, but the difference wouldn't affect the outcome. They couldn't outrun this thing. If Eric had ever wanted to see Mr. Smith, it was right now. Not wanting to witness his own gory end, he closed his eyes.

Just as the claws reached out for Eric, a piercing whistle seemed to split his head. It forced him to his knees, clutching his temples. Just when he thought he couldn't stand it any more, it stopped. Opening his eyes, he was amazed to see the velociraptor staggering about the clearing in pain and confusion. As he watched, an apparently human figure stepped out of the underbrush and walked towards the beast. When it was about ten feet away, the figure calmly waved its arms above its head as if shooing chickens on the farm. Cowed, the deadly predator stumbled off into the trees.

Eric could feel Rose clinging to his waist and hear Sally panting with terror beside him. As he watched in awe, the figure turned and came towards them. Feeling the responsibility of being the oldest and smartest of his little group, he struggled to his feet to meet this new experience. The figure was only about five feet in height and slightly built. It had a head, two arms and two legs, but there the resemblance to a human stopped.

The creature was mostly a dark greenish colour, although the neck, insides of the arms and belly were a paler hue. Each hand had only three fingers, but they were long and delicate, and obviously capable of fine grasping actions. It stood balanced on three splayed toes. The forehead was domed, the chin virtually non-existent, despite the protruding lower part of the face. The mouth was lipless and fixed in an unnerving, permanent smile, but it was the eyes

which commanded attention. They were set on each side of a flattish nose and were large and bright yellow, with an oval black pupil. They regarded Eric with calm interest and obvious intelligence.

The only action that occurred to Eric was to pat himself on the chest theatrically and say his name two or three times. It felt stupid even as he was doing it, and this was confirmed by a nervous chuckle from Rose. However, the visitor failed to see the humour. Looking straight at Eric, it opened its wide mouth and said, "Eric."

The sound was high pitched and somewhere between a whistle and a bird-call, but it was recognizably Eric's name.

"It can talk," said Eric in amazement.

"It can tawk," mimicked the creature in its whistling, bird-like voice.

"Rose," said Eric pointing at his sister.

"Rose," came the response.

"Sally." The dog wagged its tail at the sound of its name.

"Sa"y."

"It seems to have trouble with 'l'," said Eric. He pointed to the green chest in front of him. Patting itself on the chest as Eric had done a few moments before, it uttered a low whistling sound. It sounded like a large bird call — weet, weet.

"I don't know if Weet is your name, the name of your tribe or your species," said Eric helplessly, "but thank you very much for saving us."

Weet inclined his head slightly, as if trying to make

sense of the strange noises he was hearing.

"Ask him for something to eat." The practical side of Rose was taking over again.

"We don't know if his food would poison us or not."

"Oh, Eric. It doesn't matter. If we don't eat, we'll starve to death here anyway."

Weet watched and listened to this exchange with apparent interest. Eric sighed and tried his sign language again. Patting his stomach and pointing down his throat, he hoped Weet had a similar digestive system.

Still with no apparent expression on his face, Weet turned and walked away. After a few steps he turned and looked back.

"He wants us to follow him," said Rose triumphantly.

Weet turned again and slowly led them into the trees.

As they walked, Eric found comfort in talking. "You know, I think I've seen Weet before."

"How could you?" Rose was doubtful. "We've never been here before. Was he in one of your dreams?"

"No, but there's a picture in one of my books. Someone made a model of what he thought dinosaurs might have evolved into if they hadn't died out. It looked a lot like Weet, but it was just guesswork. No one realized that they could have evolved into this before they died out."

"Hasn't anyone found his bones?" Rose seemed unconcerned that the green figure in front of them should have turned to stone long ago.

"No," Eric replied thoughtfully. "Maybe his bones are too fragile to be preserved, or maybe there aren't very many of them."

"How old do you think he is?" Rose's question surprised Eric.

"Sixty-five million and something," he replied, with more flippancy than he felt.

"No, I mean is he an adult or a child like us?"

That was something Eric hadn't thought of. Perhaps Weet was just a playful child and his father was bigger with less of a sense of humour. He pushed that uncomfortable thought out of his mind.

This was strange, very strange. Weet was glad that they were walking now. It gave him a chance to think. He had found the mimicry tiring. What were these creatures? He hadn't stopped to look when he had seen the sickleclaw attacking them. They did look different. He assumed that they were from another tribe, but he had never heard of a tribe like this. Certainly, they wore second skins like the homs, but that was where the resemblance ended.

Two of these new creatures were quite disgusting — short, stubby and a sickly pale colour, with voices like the guttural calls of the swamp crocodiles. But it was the smell that was the worst. It was bitter and sweet at the same time, rather like the odour from the marat burrows, but not as earthy and much stronger. It was all he could do to stop himself from covering his nose, but that would have been unforgivable and, besides, the smell wasn't too bad now that they were moving.

The third one smelled different, not as strong and more like the marats. In fact, it looked a little like a marat, but it was too large and marats never came out in the open in broad daylight. It didn't talk much either. Perhaps it was a pet like Sinor.

The thought of Sinor waiting back at home made Weet sad. He had been looking forward to this walkabout as a chance to get away from his parents and to have some time doing things on his own. Just to be able to get up and walk wherever he wanted, whenever he wanted, without having any chores to do or hatchlings to watch over, was something he had craved. He had also been looking forward to getting away from all the gloomy talk about the changes. It seemed to be the only thing the adults cared about these days and he was bored by it. But things hadn't worked out quite as he had planned.

The first couple of days had been fine. The sense of freedom had overcome everything else. He had taken such pleasure in being the master of his own destiny that he had not thought about anything outside his immediate environment. The third day was different. He was idly eating a piece of fruit when, without thinking, he had held out a bit to Sinor, but no one was there. He had suddenly felt an overwhelming sense of loneliness. He missed Sinor, he missed his parents and his home, he even missed the hatchlings, but not very much.

On that day, he also began to notice things around

him. He noticed how the fruit was just a little bit too small for the time of year, he noticed how the leaves on the trees and bushes seemed to droop a little more than usual and then he noticed the sick shovelbill. It was staggering around in a clearing, obviously in the last stages of illness. The colour was almost completely gone from the flap of skin which ran down from its long, curved crest and its breathing came in irregular booming gasps. Surprisingly, the sickleclaws had not found it yet, but several brightly coloured ovis sat in the surrounding trees preening themselves and picking their teeth in anticipation.

What was most surprising was that the shovelbill was alone. Weet had seen sick ones before, but they had always been surrounded by other members of the herd who brought the sick beast food and tried to prevent it from falling over. In fact, shovelbills had been known to delay their migrations for several days while they attended to a sick herd member. They would not leave until the sick animal recovered or died. But here was one obviously very sick and completely alone.

As if all that hadn't been enough, in the evening, while he had been looking for a place to build his night-nest, he had seen a couple of homs. They had been a long way off, but they were travelling in the same direction as he was. Of course, they were mounted on shovelbills and could move much faster than he could, but they didn't seem to be in any hurry. Weet didn't think they had seen him but, to be on the safe side, he had taken special care to build a well-hidden nest.

The sight of the homs and their shovelbills had made Weet think about the importance of his task. If he could bring back an egg, and if it hatched successfully, then his family might be able to rear and train the hatchling. Eventually, they too might have shovelbills to ride, just like the homs.

Weet had fallen asleep to images of himself riding shovelbills to far off places. Later in the night, he had been troubled by strange dreams and had woken the next morning feeling cold, miserable and alone. Weet thought a lot in the following days, about his family, himself and his world. Maybe that was the real purpose behind the strict instructions his parents had given him about which nesting site he was to take the egg from, the way he was to get there and the length of time he was to stay away. They were all just ways to make sure he had time to think. Well, he had done the thinking, though he hadn't come up with any answers. Soon, he would get the egg and head home.

The only problem was these odd creatures he had saved. By the right of saving, they were his, but he wasn't sure he wanted them. They weren't his people, they smelled and they didn't even know how to look after themselves. Yet, Weet was glad of their company. They were friendly enough and learning about them distracted him. What would happen if he took them home, he didn't know. He was only a day away by the direct route so he didn't have long to think about it. First he had to concentrate on getting the egg and keeping these new creatures out of trouble. Growing up was turning out to be a lot harder than he had expected.

CHAPTER 6

Lunch

Weet stopped Eric and Rose in a thick patch of bushes. The bushes were laden with fruit of various kinds. There were the brown, round ones they had seen before, but also some yellow ones that looked remarkably like oranges. On thin creepers growing around some of the tree-trunks hung green banana-like fruit.

Weet picked off a yellow fruit, peeled back the thin skin and took a bite."Ornj," he said, offering a piece to Eric. Feeling more than a little nervous, Eric took a small nibble. The taste was bitter, but not unpleasant. "Thank you," he said.

Weet broke off a second piece and offered it to Rose.

"Go ahead," said Eric, "it's not too bad."

Rose took an experimental bite. "Yech, it's sour." Rose screwed up her face in distaste.

"You were the one who was complaining about being hungry. Unless you want to gnaw bones with

Sally, this is probably all we can get. And be polite."

The thought of gnawing a dinosaur bone was more disgusting than eating the sour fruit.

"Thank you," said Rose and continued nibbling glumly.

Weet handed a third piece to Sally. "Yech, it's sour," he said. Eric and Rose burst our laughing. Sally, nose turned up in disgust, retreated to search for more bones. This was not a problem. On their way to the fruit bushes, they had all seen a lot of bones of all shapes and sizes scattered over the ground. There were so many that Sally had given up trying to carry the tastiest ones with her.

The three strange friends settled down on the ground to lunch on the yellow fruit. Sally soon joined them with a respectable bone. Between mouthfuls, Eric and Rose took turns teaching Weet words. His capacity to mimic and remember seemed limitless. Everything came out in the same whistling tones, but his only real problem seemed to be an inability to pronounce the letter "l". Thus, clothes became "c'othes," and leaf "'eaf." However, "fruit," "branch," "bush," "bone" and "dog" were all rapidly added to his growing vocabulary. They even managed to teach Weet "mother" and "father." "Sister" was a special favourite and he took relish in repeating it.

In return, Weet taught them that the green fruit was called "nans" and the brown "apps."

After about a quarter of an hour, they had eaten all they could manage of the bitter fruit. Eric was torturing himself with the thought of his mother's blueberry pie with a large scoop of ice cream, when they were interrupted by a loud crashing nearby. Eric and Rose looked at each other worriedly, but Weet appeared unconcerned. Putting down his fruit, he began crawling through the bushes in the direction of the noise. Eric and Rose followed, with Sally close at their heels.

They stopped at the edge of their clump of trees. In the open area in front of them was scattered a herd of the largest animals they had ever seen. There were about twenty of them, ranging in size from babies little bigger than Eric to giants more than fifteen feet tall. Most were crouching down, resting on their shorter forelegs while they cropped low plants and ferns. A few were rearing up on their hind legs to tear down tree branches. In either case, they used their long, stiff tails for balance. Each creature also had a long crest extending back from its head, from which was draped a brightly coloured flap of skin.

"Hadrosaurs," whispered Eric. "Parasaurolophus, judging from the the crests. Look at those skin flaps attached to the crests. The colours are recognition signals. See the way the skin is stretched when it lowers its head? And look, the smaller ones with the duller skin flaps must be the females."

He was engrossed with a scene which he had only imagined until now. "Listen, they're calling. That's what the crests are for. They're filled with air tubes that help make the sound."

The clearing was filled with grunts and howls as the creatures moved about feeding. As Eric watched the scene, he became more and more puzzled. "What's the matter?" asked Rose. "Will they attack us?"

"No, no, they're plant eaters. See those large beaks. They're for cropping the tough plants which are then ground up by hundreds of flat teeth at the back of the mouth. Anyway, Weet's whistling would probably stop them if they came this way. I was just wondering why there seem to be so many sick ones."

Sure enough, when Rose began looking past the sheer size of the animals, quite a number of them did appear to be sick. They moved more slowly and often had to rest. Off to the right, one was very ill. Its colour was not the yellowish green of the healthy members of the herd, but a pale grey pallor. It could hardly lift its massive head to reach even the lower branches of the trees.

Eric tapped Weet on the shoulder. He pointed out a few of the sickest-looking animals, shrugged his shoulders and put a questioning look on his face. He had to repeat the gesture a number of times, before Weet understood. Weet clutched his arms around his chest and began to shake.

"Cold?" said Eric.

Weet pointed up to the sun and repeated the shivering gesture.

"He's telling us they're cold," repeated Eric thoughtfully. "Maybe the climate's changing and the cold is making them sick."

As if in response to his words, the notes of the hadrosaur calls changed. They became more urgent and high-pitched and the herd began to mill around in confusion. From a clump of trees off to their right, five velociraptors appeared. They moved slowly round the edge of the clearing, watching the milling herd. Their sunken bellies added an extra dimension of urgency to their fearsome array of teeth and claws.

Without any apparent pattern to their circling, the velociraptors were gradually isolating the very sick hadrosaur from the others. Its calls became frantic.

With surprising speed and agility, the velociraptor pack attacked. They were much smaller than the hadrosaur, but their method of attack doomed the sick beast from the start. One by one, as they spotted an opening, each velociraptor would break away from the encircling group to lunge at the prey. Jumping ten or twelve feet into the air, each would strike a fast blow with the claws on its hind legs. Soon the hadrosaur's flanks were torn and bloody.

The hadrosaur tried to defend itself by swinging its massive tail from side to side, but the velociraptors easily evaded its feeble swipes. It had no chance. Very quickly, loss of blood and illness weakened the poor beast. Once the claws reached the vulnerable neck and head, the struggle would be over. The attackers would gorge themselves and all that would be left would be a pile of bones to excite a paleontologist who wouldn't be born for 65 million years.

Gesturing silently at the children, Weet retreated back into the bushes.

"Poor thing." Rose was close to tears.

"It wouldn't have lasted long anyway," said Eric. "You saw how sick it was. I wonder if the cold was killing it. If it was cold-blooded, like a snake, it would need warm weather to survive. It couldn't keep itself warm the way we can by turning our food into energy. Of course, it wouldn't have needed as much food as

we do, and its large size would mean that small changes in temperature wouldn't bother it. But if it started to get really cold, cold enough for its body to cool down even a little, it would have a lot of trouble warming up again."

"But it feels warm," said Rose, "warmer than at home."

"Yeah, but there's a chill in the air, and it probably gets pretty cold at night. Maybe it's got to the stage where it's so cold at night that the hadrosaurs lose more heat than they can regain from the sun during the following day. But that doesn't make sense. A lot of scientists think these creatures were warm-blooded."

"Maybe it needs sunscreen?" suggested Rose.

"What?" Eric looked at his sister with a puzzled frown.

"Maybe the sun is making it sick just like it will make us sick if we don't wear sunscreen when we play outside."

Eric's frown turned to a look of amazement. "Yeah," he said, "you could be right. If the ozone is thinning in this world too, then the UV radiation might be making them sick," he laughed. "Maybe the dinosaurs died of sunburn. And then maybe I didn't understand Weet and the cold is unrelated to the sickness. Or maybe the cold is just stressing them out so much that they are getting sick in the same way Mom says we'll get sick if we go out on a wet day without jackets. Either way, the climate seems to be changing and the dinosaurs are getting sick."

"But those veloci-things don't seem to be getting sick." Rose shuddered at the memory. "Maybe their feathers are protecting them."

"Could be," Eric agreed. "They must be warm-blooded. There's no point in having feathers unless you can make your own heat. I doubt the cold would bother them. But it wouldn't really matter. If all the hadrosaurs died, the velociraptors would die out too, because there would be no more food. And what about Weet? He doesn't have feathers and he's pretty active. He must be warm-blooded."

Eric fell silent. Being here was fascinating, but this world was turning out to be a lot more complex than he had imagined.

Weet led his three companions in a wide circle around the agitated shovelbills and the feasting sickleclaws; more sick shovelbills. The shivering sickness was getting worse. Weet was beginning to worry that the sickness was so bad that the shovelbills might not be nesting this season. How then would he get an egg to complete his walkabout? He would have to hurry. Feeding these creatures had slowed him down and, if he was going to reach home tomorrow, he would have to find the egg this afternoon.

He hoped the creatures would not slow him down too much. They did not know enough to keep quiet when sickleclaws were around. If they couldn't whistle and didn't keep quiet, they couldn't have been around long. And yet they seemed to know the shovelbills. What had they called them? Parasaurolophus, hadrosaurs? Odd words, but then their language was odd.

Weet wondered if the one called Eric had understood what he had said. He seemed to be asking about the shivering sickness, which had started just when the nights began to get cold. He had seemed satisfied with the answer, but there was no way of knowing whether he had understood. Weet wasn't sure if he himself understood what was causing the sickness. He would have to work at learning more of their words. In his mind, he experimented:

"Poor thing. Wi" they attack us? Co'd. Hadrosaurs... Skin f'aps... C'imate changing... dinosaurs getting sick."

He didn't understand much of it yet, but he was beginning to put some words together and he was starting to realize that the odd expressions that passed across their faces when they spoke meant something too. If he concentrated, he could memorize the sounds. It was fun, rather like learning his own language had been, or picking up the stories of his people's past from his father.

Weet glanced up at the sky. It was getting late. They would have to hurry. As they walked along, he touched the largest of his three new companions on the arm. They had very strange skin, these creatures. It felt smooth to the touch and was loose like the belly skin on a hungry sickleclaw. But the skin of these creatures was loose all over and didn't fill out when they ate. As the one called Eric looked at him, he pointed up at the sun again.

This time, he drew his hand across the sky towards the horizon and did his shivering act again. When he repeated the motion, Eric's eyes lit up.

"He's telling us that it gets cold at night. See, I was right."

Weet was beginning to understand. "He" seemed to be another word for himself, "us" was all of them together, "cold" was the change and "night" was, well, just night.

"See, I was right." His mimicry pleased them. Soon he might be able to talk to them. There was so much he wanted to ask.

But right now they had to hurry on. There were still several hours until dark, but they would have to find somewhere to stop by then, before it got cold. The cold wasn't bad enough to make Weet sick, but it disturbed his sleep and he would wake up tired and lethargic. Often he wanted just to burrow down into his sleeping nest and lie there all day. One night he had woken up early to find marats running over him. He had chased them away, but the memory of their smooth furry forms running over him as he slept had spoiled his sleep for several nights.

After that, he had had the idea of catching them and making himself a second skin like the homs did. Perhaps then the nights would not seem so cold. The trouble was the marats were small and fast. That made them difficult to catch. They weren't bothered by his whistling, so he had to rush around trying to pick them up with his hands or dig down into their burrows, and that was all very tiring. After a full day and night, he had only caught two, and received a nasty bite from the sharp teeth of one of them. If only the shovelbills were covered with fur!

"Sally, come here!" Weet's thoughts were interrupted by Eric recalling the large marat-like one from a very stale-looking bone with some flesh still attached. These creatures just didn't know how to keep quiet. They were continually talking and crashing through the undergrowth on those clumsy feet of theirs. It would be just his luck if they brought a whole pack of sickleclaws down on them. He would have to leave them well out of the way when he went for the egg. Couldn't be far now. Already they were at the ford in the river. All they had to do was cross and cut back down to the beach. As they waded through the shallow water, small crocodile-like creatures splashed away from them and crawled up the banks.

About an hour after crossing the river, Weet stopped and cocked his head to one side. Yes, there it was, unmistakable, the sound of the water. He hurried forward up a small rise and lay down to peer through some spikes of grass. There they were, covering the small low promontory off to the left. Shovelbills, not the kind that the homs rode, but these always seemed more placid and would probably be easier to train. If he worked his way along the bank, then it would only be a short dash out to collect an egg from a nest at the edge of the colony and then back into the grass. With a lot of crashing and panting, the three strangers came up and flopped down beside Weet. What a noise! He really would have to keep them out of the way.

CHAPTER 7

The Nesting Site

The scene that met Eric's eyes as he pushed through the coarse grass took his breath away. It was similar to the one they had seen from the tunnel, but the tide was in now and waves lapped along a sandy beach a mere twenty feet away. The high-tide line was marked by a collection of driftwood, seaweed and curved fragments of shell. The pieces of shell had a pearly lustre and glowed in the sunlight.

Slightly to Eric's right and just below them, two animals were strolling along the beach. They were about the size of cows, with short legs and low-slung, squat bodies. Their tails were long and ended in a pair of bony lumps which must have made a fearsome club-like weapon if the animal ever got angry. The front legs were shorter than the rear and that, combined with the small head, gave the impression that they were continuously walking downhill.

But it was the creatures' armour that really caught Eric's attention and gave him the impression that he was looking at a couple of small tanks. The backs of these strange beasts were covered with hard plates, each of which had a bony knob protruding from its centre. Along the sides of their heads and down their flanks, rows of vicious spikes jutted out. The spikes were longest on the shoulder, where they reached almost two feet and curved forward threateningly. Altogether, they looked frightening, but they plodded ponderously along, showing no interest in the group.

"Ankylosaurs," he muttered, and had no sooner said it than his attention was caught by an even more extraordinary scene.

Along the beach to the left, a large promontory jutted out into the water. It was wide and flat and completely covered with two-feet high mounds which were topped with caps of vegetation. Each mound was about 30 feet away from its nearest neighbour and most of the space between them was filled with resting hadrosaurs. They were like the parasaurolophus they had seen earlier, but without the long, swept-back crest. These just had a small bony lump on the forehead between the eyes. The lumps were bright red and, combined with the broad duck-like bill, gave the animals a vaguely stupid look. An assortment of low grunts and grumblings and the smell of rotting vegetation filled the air.

"Ugh! What a horrible smell!" Rose had never been one to hide how she felt.

"Shh..." Eric caught the glance that Weet shot at Rose. "We don't want to disturb them," he whispered. "There must be over a hundred. Maiasaura I would guess, just like Egg Island in Montana. Those mounds are the nests. The parents are too big to sit on them, so they cover the eggs with rotting plants to keep them warm until it's time for them to hatch. That's what's causing the smell. It's incredible. I wonder why Weet has brought us here?"

As they watched, an occasional hadrosaur would appear from somewhere inland and cross out to the colony. Amid a chorus of protesting grunts, it would pick its way through the nests as carefully as its three tons would allow. At the mounds, these new arrivals would regurgitate more vegetation on top of the nests before settling down beside their mates. Eric had an impression of continuous motion, but it was slow and irregular and didn't appear threatening in any way.

"Ooh! Gross!" Rose whispered. She was still disgusted, but at least now she was expressing it quietly.

Weet made motions with his hands which obviously meant that they were to stay where they were. Then he slithered back down the bank and began to work his way along towards the promontory.

"Where's he going?" Rose asked nervously. "I don't want to be left alone."

Eric contained his desire to point out that Rose wasn't alone, mainly because he knew what she meant. In this world, without Weet to help them, they would be alone. Alone, scared and in great danger.

"I don't know," he responded. "Let's follow him."

"He told us to stay here." Rose sounded uncertain.

"Yes, but if we stay out of sight, he'll never know."

"O.K.," Rose agreed.

The three of them set off after Weet, keeping him

just in sight through the grass.

Weet worked his way along the beach ridge until he was opposite the promontory. There was a well-beaten path here where the hadrosaurs came and went. Crouching down in the grass, Weet waited and, behind him, Eric, Rose and Sally waited too.

After a few minutes, heavy footsteps announced the return of another hadrosaur. As it passed, Weet darted up and fell into step beside one of the huge back legs. He used an odd half-skip, half-jump to keep in step, but he was so close to the trunk-like limb that he was very difficult to see. As the great beast reached the first nests, Weet suddenly fell to the side and rolled into position flat beside a nest, but on the far side of the mound from the resting parent. He lay there while the commotion caused by the returning animal died down and then, extremely slowly, began to reach into the nest.

After what seemed an eternity to the watching Eric, Weet had extended an arm under the foul vegetation. To be able to reach completely over the wide lip of the mound, he almost had to stand up. Eric felt sure the hadrosaur must see Weet, but nothing disturbed the tranquillity of the scene. As Weet slowly withdrew his arm, Eric and Rose gasped. Cupped in Weet's long, delicate fingers was an egg, slightly larger than a softball and a very pale, almost pearly grey colour. Even at that distance, the surface of the egg appeared translucent and reflected the pale sunlight in a rainbow of muted colour.

"It's beautiful," sighed Rose.

Even Weet seemed impressed. He paused to gaze at

the almost glowing globe in his hand. In that split second, chaos erupted around him. From behind a nest to Weet's right darted a small, skinny, ostrich-like animal. It was about Weet's height, but most of that was taken up with a long, slender neck and a rigid, balancing tail. The neck was topped by a narrow head with a long-toothed jaw and two impossibly wide, yellow eyes. The creature was running on its hind legs while, between its forefeet, it clutched an egg. Like Weet, it was stealing but, unlike him, it relied on speed rather than stealth to escape.

The moment it sprang up, the maiasauras reacted. Amid an incredible bellowing, about twenty creatures on the landward tip of the peninsula rose to their feet. With extraordinary agility, the egg-stealer darted between the mounds and headed for the beach. Weet turned to follow, but he was too slow. The maiasaura on the far side of the nest rose and turned to watch the fleeing predator. As it did so, its great tail swept over the nest and caught Weet on the shoulder. It was only the tip of the tail, but it was enough to catapult Weet head-over-heels for about ten feet, where he lay still as the egg rolled gently into a hollow beside him.

"WEET!" Rose's scream echoed across the bizarre landscape.

Eric was paralyzed. If Weet stayed there, he would surely be trampled by the milling hadrosaurs. But what could he do to help? To go down there would be to risk being trampled too. To stay would condemn them to watching their new friend die.

Already the closest hadrosaur had noticed Weet and the egg and was moving round the nest toward

him. Eric's agony of indecision was resolved when Rose pushed past him and headed at full speed down the beach. Without a second thought, Eric set off after her.

Rose was almost three-quarters of the way to the still-prone Weet and Eric had nearly drawn level with his flying sister, when a brown blur shot past them both. Without slowing, Sally leapt over the fallen Weet and faced the advancing maiasaura. Slowing only to bare her teeth and growl, Sally raced back and forth barking furiously. Her antics seemed to confuse the dinosaur, which stopped and moved its head from side to side, as if trying to decide what to make of this strange, dancing creature in front of it.

With a fervent wish that tiny brains take a long time to adjust to the unusual, Eric grabbed Weet under the shoulders and hauled. The surprising lightness of the body and a healthy respect for a maiasaura's foot produced an impressive rate of retreat back up the beach. Since he had to run backwards in order to drag Weet, Eric could see what was going on. Rose was following closely with the egg clutched protectively in her arms. Farther back, Sally, still barking, was conducting a strategic withdrawal. The egg-stealer had vanished and the maiasauras, though still unsettled and restless, showed no signs of undertaking a pursuit.

As soon as they were hidden within the long grass, Eric laid Weet down and sat heavily in the sand. He was gasping for breath and his chest hurt. Weet wasn't moving and his eyes were closed.

"Is he dead?" asked Rose between panting breaths.

"How should I know?" Eric sounded more brusque than he intended, but the thought of Weet being dead, or too seriously injured for them to help, scared him. He watched the pale green chest intently. It seemed to be rising and falling.

"He seems to be breathing. Maybe he's just unconscious," Eric hoped out loud.

"Should we keep him warm or something?"

"Yes, and let's make him a nice cup of tea, too." Rose recoiled at the harshness in her brother's tone. "And anyway, what were you doing running off like that?" he continued. "You could have got us killed."

"Weet needed help," she answered defensively. "If we had sat around discussing it, he would have been squashed."

"Well, don't ever run off like that again," Eric snapped at Rose, even though he knew she was right. His anger was really at himself for being indecisive. How could he have even considered not helping Weet? After all, they owed him their lives. He felt tense and confused. Why did he have to be the eldest? Why did he have to have the responsibility for making decisions? A warm feeling on his hand distracted him and he looked down. Sally was licking his palm.

"You were great, old girl," he said, relaxing and reaching out to scratch her behind the ear. "That dinosaur had never seen anything like you before."

"Look, he's opening his eyes." The joy in Rose's voice was undisguised. All at once, the tension of the last hour was released as she wept uncontrollably.

The first thing Weet became aware of were the alien voices arguing above him. What kind of a dream was this? Then he opened his eyes and remembered his strange new companions. The one called Rose was making odd noises and water was flowing out of her eyes. He couldn't even begin to think what that meant. He moved and a sharp pain shot through his right shoulder. He lay back and tried to remember.

The egg! He had been going after the egg. And he had got one too, a beautiful one just about to hatch. Then the egg-stealer had appeared. Like him, it must have been hiding behind a mound. The shovelbills had panicked and the close one had hit him with its tail. That was all he could remember. How did he get up here in the grass? His friends must have rescued him.

Weet looked around at his three companions. Rose and Eric were out of breath and were looking at him with those funny, rubbery faces of theirs. Sally was lying down, apparently asleep. He owed them his life. They had repaid their debt and the four of them were now bound together forever. Painfully, Weet sat up and cupped his hands in the traditional greeting posture.

"Thank you," he said slowly.

A new stream of tears flowed out of Rose's eyes. "You're welcome," she managed through sobs. Reaching behind her, she picked up the egg and placed it in Weet's hands.

How strange! They had even saved the egg. Weet looked down at it. It was perfect, perhaps only a couple of days from hatching. Through the subtle colours reflected in the leathery skin, he could even make out the curled form of the baby shovelbill. If he could keep it warm tonight, he should be home with it by tomorrow evening.

Weet felt a chill breeze rustle the grass. He looked up. The sun was getting low. They couldn't stay here for the night. They would have to move inland and find a place to build a sleeping nest.

Slowly, Weet stood up. Tucking the egg under his painful right arm, he silently beckoned for them to follow. The brown one was still lying in the sand.

"Sa"y, come here."

Weet was glad to see Eric and Rose making the funny choking sounds that seemed to indicate that they were happy. In silence, Sally hauled herself up to follow them away from the nesting site.

Weet led the small group inland for about an hour. The ground was rising gently and the vegetation was becoming less dense. This was far enough, and there were plenty of fruit bushes around to eat from. That clump of tall firs would do. They stood on a slight rise, so the ground would be dry, and there would be none of the low bushes that the marats liked to burrow under, so their sleep wouldn't be disturbed.

Working as quickly as he could in the cooling air, Weet began to gather the soft underbranches of the silal bushes. The bushes were far apart and, for four of them, they would need a lot of branches. After a few moments of watching, Eric and Rose also began collecting and soon they had a respectable pile at the foot of the largest tree. Weet divided the pile into four and arranged them into sleeping mats in a crude circle. Beside his pile, he scooped out a small hollow into which he placed the egg before covering it with a thick layer of silal.

Next, he began going around collecting food. There were no ornj bushes here, but there were lots of the long nans hanging from the tree-creepers and some brown apps. Again, Eric and Rose helped him and soon they had a pile of fruit in the centre of the circle.

Weet sat down on his bed. That should do. Now, with luck, they would get a good rest and be home tomorrow. Distractedly, he picked up a nan and began to eat. The sun was almost touching the horizon and the temperature was dropping noticeably. What a strange day it had been. What would tomorrow hold in store? Weet finished his fruit, lay down and pulled some silal over himself. The others were still eating. He hoped it wouldn't get too cold.

CHAPTER 8

Night-time

"I guess this is our hotel room," said Eric with a pitiful attempt at humour. "It could use a coat of paint."

He was sitting on his bed of branches, peeling a nan. They were much sweeter than the yellow round ones they had had for lunch, but they tasted floury and left a coating on the tongue. Still, they were preferable to the apps which were slimy and smelled vaguely of cheap perfume.

It was almost dark now and the chill in the air reminded Eric of pleasant fall evenings which held the promise of harsh frosts to come. Weet had been very silent ever since they had left the nesting site. Now he was curled up in his vegetative mat, apparently asleep. Eric supposed that his shoulder was causing him problems. He hoped nothing was broken. Weet's bones must be very fragile, judging by how easy it had been to drag him up the beach.

Eric had seen lots of broken dinosaur bones, and he had even glued a few together, but he had no idea how to fix one on a live dinosaur. No, not a dinosaur; a friend. After all that had happened to them during the day, Eric could no longer think of Weet as a dinosaur. Despite all the recent discoveries about dinosaurs, the word still implied slowness and stupidity, neither of which applied to Weet. It was also a word from Eric's time, not Weet's. Now that they seemed stuck in Weet's time, it appeared wrong.

"What do you think Mom and Dad are doing now?" Rose interrupted him with her own train of thought. "Do you suppose they are looking for us?"

"Of course, they are," Eric replied. "They must be worried sick by now." He imagined his mother and father calling them for lunch. There would have been no reply, so they would have looked around the hoodoos. They would have become increasingly worried and eventually driven into town for the police. Perhaps there had been time to launch a search of the badlands before dark. His parents were probably back in some local hotel, unable to sleep, just waiting for the morning to continue the search.

Eric shivered, not from the cold but at a bizarre thought that had settled in his mind. Suppose they didn't get back? Suppose they were permanently stuck here at the end of the Cretaceous? Eventually, they would die here, either as a velociraptor's lunch or of old age. Either way, their parents would have spent the afternoon looking in vain for their children when, all the time, they were literally underfoot, buried in rock 65 million-years-old. Eric decided not to mention his thoughts to Rose.

"Don't worry, Rose." Eric tried to sound positive. "We'll get home somehow. Judging from where the sun went down, Weet is leading us west, so we must be almost following the highway back to Calgary. If there's one tunnel, there must be others. We'll find one and be back soon. Anyway, we should try and get some sleep. Who knows how far we may have to go tomorrow."

Rose yawned and lay down.

"Good night, Eric," she mumbled. "I hope you're right."

"So do I," Eric wished under his breath. Then, more loudly, "Good night, Rose. Sleep well."

"Good night, Ericrosesa''y," Weet's voice came from the shadowy pile across the circle.

"Good night, Weet," they both replied. "And thanks again," added Rose.

Eric lay on his back and looked at the stars. The Milky Way curved across the blackness above him with almost unnatural brightness. In this whole world, there was not a single artificial light to dull the sky's display. Even the wispy cloud which seemed to diffuse the sunlight so much appeared to have no effect on the stars. But something was wrong. Where was Cassiopeia's Chair? It should be right above him. Eric tilted his head to look north; no Big Dipper either. He looked south; no Orion. Lots of stars, but not a single familiar one.

Of course, the sky above the dinosaurs would have been different. Eric remembered reading that the Milky Way galaxy took more than 200 million years to

spin around once. So, in 65 million years it would have gone through more than a quarter of a revolution and carried the earth and the sun with it. Eric chuckled quietly to himself. He had talked to Rose about walking towards Calgary. He was looking into space from a position billions of miles away from where Calgary and the rest of the earth would be.

The heavens were his. He could create and name constellations. He let his eye wander over the unfamiliar vista. There was a long line of bright stars with three curving off from one end. He would call that one the Hockey Stick constellation. There was a group in a diamond shape, the Blue Jay constellation. There were three together, a bright one with fainter ones on either side that could be the Ericrosesa"y constellation.

Eric began to tire of the game. Its reminder of where they were was depressing, and that last constellation reminded him of another worry that was nibbling at the edge of his mind. He had assumed that he was the bright star in the middle. A mere twelve hours ago, he would have thought that he was obviously the oldest, smartest and most worthy. Now it became a symbol of the heavy responsibility he felt. It was his job to look after Rose. That was almost the last thing his mother had said to him, when he went off into the hoodoos a lifetime ago.

"Don't go too far, and keep an eye on Rose." What a joke!

Being the older child, Eric had always had some looking after to do:

"Keep an eye on your sister."

"Let me know if she goes near the top of the stairs."

"Don't let Rose go up to the road."

But "Don't let Rose get eaten by a velociraptor" was one he had never considered. And was there even any point in looking after her, or himself for that matter? They seemed to be stuck here and the thought scared him. For all the times Eric had imagined this world, it was turning out to be frighteningly alien. Everything was different. The colours, the sounds, the smells, the night sky — they were all wrong and made it impossible to ever forget how far away they all were from home and whether it would be possible to get back. Even if they could somehow find a tunnel, there was no guarantee it would work in the other direction, and what would they find if it did? Would they crawl out onto the Alberta badlands only to find a world of darkness and terror?

The meteor that had sent them into the tunnel might have been huge. Eric knew that the one which had finally ended the dinosaurs' reign had been about ten kilometres across. If the one he had seen had been that size,what would his world be like now? If the meteor had landed close, say around Calgary, there would be nothing left. At the moment it had hit, Drumheller would have been on the edge of a crater that went most of the way through the earth's crust and waves of molten rock would have washed over it.

If it had landed farther away, say, somewhere in B.C., they would have had a spectacular but brief display. The shock wave would have flattened everything and the debris would have buried the landscape beneath several feet of crushed and tortured rock. Even if the big one had landed far off in the Pacific Ocean, that would only have given his home a brief respite. A rolling, dark cloud, blacker than any night, would have swept over them, and from it would have rained hot, semi-molten droplets of rock. Anything burnable would have caught fire, shedding a weird, dancing illumination on the landscape.

After the fires, it would have become cold, since not a single ray of sunlight would be able to penetrate the cloud of dust covering the earth. There would be bitter cold and total blackness for months. Whatever survived the impact and the fires would still be doomed. Eric didn't want to go back to a world like that. But would he be any better off here? He looked over at Weet's sleeping form. What kind of future did he have? A tear formed in the corner of his eye.

Eric rolled on to his side. The moon was coming up over a low hill. Even the moon was wrong. It was far too big and moving too fast and, perhaps worst of all, the friendly old man's face wasn't there. Eric closed his eyes to stop the tears, but they leaked out anyway and dripped onto his pillow of branches and moss.

Eventually, Eric fell into a disturbed sleep. The last things he noticed were Rose crawling onto his mat and snuggling up behind him and a large furry lump worming its way into the warm curve formed by his body. In a warm huddle, the only three mammals in the entire world larger than mice fell asleep.

CHAPTER 9

Awakening

Eric awoke from his dreamless sleep because his toes were cold. His mother must have come in in the night and opened his window again. She was a fresh-air freak. One day he would catch pneumonia. That would teach her. He pulled his knees up as far as the still-sleeping dog would allow and wiggled his toes. His runners were getting tight; he would need a new pair soon.

Runners? Why was he wearing runners in bed, and what was that sharp pain in his side? Reaching under his ribs, he pulled out a small branch. In a rush the memories of the previous day came flooding back. Eric opened his eyes. It was all true. There, in the pale, cold light of dawn was the alien shape of Weet and behind him, the landscape of a long-vanished world.

As gently as possible, Eric slithered out from between his sleeping companions. He stood up and shivered as the chill air cooled the sweat that had formed beneath his clothes in the night. He was stiff and foggy and the inside of his mouth felt like the floor under his bed at home, dry and dusty. Eric stepped out of the circle of mats and began waving his arms and jumping up and down. As he warmed up, the stiffness eased. He began looking around for some fruit to take away the foul taste in his mouth.

He had picked up a couple of nans before his gaze fell on Weet, lying asleep on his side. Overcome with curiosity, Eric crept over to his friend and began to examine the sleeping form. Weet's skin, which from a distance appeared almost scaly, was, in fact, quite smooth and not at all reptilian. Only down the line of his spine did a series of small knobs give a slightly lizard-like appearance.

The legs were thin, yet powerful, and ended in long, narrow feet. Each foot had three radiating toes ending in stubby black claws. When he walked, Weet used only his toes. What should have been the heel was carried off the ground. The heel had a small, sharp claw, which served no purpose that Eric could see. Perhaps it was the now-useless remnant of a more primitive foot. The hands had three long, flexible fingers that looked a little like the spider crabs' legs Eric had once found on the beach near his grandmother's. Where the fingernails should have been were tiny, sharp black claws. One finger was like Eric's thumb and could be used with the other two to pick up things. The hands managed to convey a sense of both delicacy and strength.

Gingerly, Eric worked his way around the sleeping

mat to look into Weet's face. The eyes were closed, but the bulging lids still managed to dominate the face. Above them, a broad expanse of forehead swept back over the domed head. In contrast, below the eyes, the rest of the facial features seemed to be competing for space. The nose hardly stuck out at all and the edges of the nostrils quivered with each of Weet's shallow breaths. Closed, the mouth was only a thin line fixed in a ghost of a smile above the almost non-existent chin.

Eric was just leaning forward to have a good look at Weet's ears, when the eyes opened. The sudden appearance of the huge, yellow orbs startled Eric. He jerked back and sat down abruptly.

"Sorry, sorry," he mumbled. "I was just... I didn't mean to..."

His excuses trailed off into embarrassed silence. Slowly, he held out one of the nans. Weet's eyes remained fixed on Eric, but he didn't move.

"Please, don't be offended. I didn't mean any harm. It's just that we're so different." Eric held out the fruit farther. Weet's eyes blinked and he struggled to sit up, a painful process.

"Are you O.K? Are you hurt? Did your fall yesterday break something?"

Eric's guilt at being caught looking at Weet was mixed with concern.

"What's the matter?" Rose's sleepy voice came from across the circle.

"I don't know," replied Eric. "Weet seems to be in pain. I hope it's just bruises from yesterday feeling stiff in the cold."

"It is cold," Rose agreed. "My feet are freezing. Even Sally's shivering. Can we have a fire?"

That was something Eric hadn't thought of.

"Good idea," he replied, reaching for his knife. "I bet this cold is unusual," he continued as he and Rose began collecting dry twigs and making a pile in the centre of the circle. "In the Cretaceous, it was, (or is), warmer than our time by several degrees and there's not the difference between the seasons or between day and night."

"You mean," asked Rose slowly, "that there's no winter here?"

"Maybe not. If there is, it's very mild. I wonder if the weather here is changing? Weet's warm-blooded, but he's still not used to the cold. Maybe it takes him longer than us to warm up and get going on a cold morning."

Eric paused and looked at Weet. He was sitting up now, eating the nan and watching the children's activity with silent interest. The pile of twigs was respectable now, but they also dragged a few larger branches closer, to feed the fire once it got going. Eric took out his camping knife and unscrewed the compass from the end of the handle. Inside was a rolled length of fishing twine, a hook and five wooden matches. He was glad he hadn't picked the Swiss Army knife last Christmas. The matches were not much to launch their life in this new world, but they were more use than the toothpick and the screwdriver he might have chosen.

Eric withdrew one of the matches and struck it on the knife's handle. With a soft hiss, the purple head burst into a yellow flame which began to work its way towards Eric's fingers. Before it got there, Eric managed to transfer it to some of the twigs, and soon the small fire was burning cheerfully. By carefully adding larger sticks, they soon had a good blaze, whose heat could be felt around the edge of the sleeping circle.

They could make fire! Eric could make fire! As he watched the yellow and orange flames devouring the sticks, Weet was overwhelmed by the sight. He felt the warmth of the flames. The stiffness left him as warmer blood loosened his muscles. His shoulder still hurt, but nothing seemed to be broken.

This was the answer. He had never before been so close to fire. It had always been something to fear, a natural phenomenon which could sweep through a home-nest in a matter of minutes, destroying everything in its path. Yet here was Eric calmly carrying it around trapped in a small stick to be released at will. With tame fire, Weet's family would never need to feel the cold again.

Weet dragged his eyes away from the hypnotizing flames and looked at Eric.

"What?" he asked tentatively, pointing at the fire. He watched as Eric's face broke into the rubbery expression that seemed to signify that he was happy.

Eric began chattering to Rose. "He just asked a question.

He wants to know what fire is. He's never seen it before.'

Eric turned and addressed Weet more slowly. "Fire," he said, "fire."

"Fire," repeated Weet, "thank you." Weet remembered that this seemed to be an important word. His gaze returned to the fire. What did this small fire feel like? He reached out a finger. It got warmer, the closer he moved it. Eventually his finger was almost touching the flames. It hurt. Weet jerked his hand back.

"It's hot, don't touch," said Rose in a perfect imitation of her mother. Weet looked around.

"What is that?" he asked, pointing at Eric's knife.

"Knife," said Eric, proceeding to take it apart and handing the pieces to Weet. "Blade, saw, compass, fishing line, hook, matches."

"Matches." So those were the fire sticks. Eric had scraped one down the side of the knife to release the fire.

"No, don't!" Eric yelled as one of the matches flared up. "Too late. We only had five, now we're down to three." He held out his hand.

These matches must be very valuable. Was this all there were? Weet watched the tiny yellow flame creep towards his fingers, as it consumed the match. So that was it. You could only use these things once.

Remembering that even when fire was trapped it could still hurt, Weet dropped the match onto the ground where it spluttered out. He placed the remaining matches in Eric's outstretched hand. If there were only these few left, it would be a disappointment, but who knew what other wonders these new creatures had brought into his world. He could hardly wait to tell his family about the extraordinary things that he had discovered.

CHAPTER 10

Home

"He's never seen fire before!" Eric marvelled. "I wish we had more matches. I shouldn't have wasted all those on the camping trip in the summer."

"Can't we just rub two sticks together?" To Rose's practical side, nothing was impossible.

"It's not quite as easy as that," replied Eric, remembering old films of hunched figures laboriously spinning sticks until a tiny piece of dried moss ignited. "But maybe I could rig up a bow with the fishing line. That would make spinning the stick easier. We can try it later."

Now that he was warmed up, Weet was busy collecting and eating fruit for breakfast.

"I hope there's more to eat here than this fruit," said Eric, as he joined him. "I'd give my right arm for a burger bar."

"Oh," breathed Rose longingly, "a hamburger."

"With fries and ketchup," added Eric.

"And a strawberry milkshake." Rose said dreamily.

Eric passed her a nan. "Here," he said teasingly, "pretend it's a banana split, covered with chocolate sauce, with a cherry on the top and ice cream on the side." He grinned wickedly.

"Eric," said Rose with a note of panic, "don't. If you go on like that, I'll never be able to eat this fruit and I'll starve to death. Then you'd be sorry."

Eric chuckled, but he didn't say anything else as he finished a couple of nans. He was wondering what this day held in store for them all.

In fact, most of the day was quite uneventful. Weet was obviously in a hurry. After collecting the egg and tucking it under his arm, he set off at a rapid pace away from the rising sun. Eric and Rose's struggle to keep up would have been hopeless except for the unusual way Weet travelled. He set a fast walking pace for a short time. Then he stopped to rest. At first, Eric thought he was allowing them to catch up, but as the day wore on, Weet's pace slowed to a speed they could match. Yet he still used the same pattern of stopping and starting. He also nibbled on fruit along the way rather than stopping for regular meals as Eric and Rose were used to.

As the day wore on, Eric noticed that the landscape was changing. They were gradually climbing, and the lusher vegetation of the coast was giving way to more open plains. There were still clumps of trees but they were farther apart and generally taller. Between them, small bushes and low, flowering shrubs carpeted the ground. The trees looked rather like the redwoods Eric had seen on their California holiday.

The only wildlife they saw were some hadrosaurs early in the day and a few small, agile predators, similar to the one that had stolen the maiasaura egg. Eric thought they might be troodontids, the dinosaur line from which the much larger and more fearsome Tyrannosaurus rex might have developed. The thought of tyrannosaurus worried him. He knew they lived around here, but their fossils were very rare so perhaps there weren't many of them. But if they did run into one, would Weet be able to whistle something that size away?

By afternoon, Eric's legs began to feel like lead and even Rose became too tired to complain. His original impression of a sparsely-populated world returned. Yet he kept having the feeling that they were being watched. He couldn't see anything, but the feeling persisted annoyingly. He supposed that it was just a result of being in such an unknown environment and that he was beginning to imagine things.

All day they headed west. During the stops, Eric would turn back and examine the view. In the distance, he could see the wide silver strip of the sea. The coastline was laid out below in a complex line of bays, peninsulas and scattered islands. Eric even thought he could recognize the peninsula where Weet had stolen the egg. Certainly there was a river flowing into the sea nearby and, if that was the one where they had washed yesterday, then the hole through which they had arrived must be just a little farther along the coast. Eric had no plan and couldn't see how returning to the hole would help them, but it might be their only link with their own time. Somehow, he felt more secure knowing that they could return to it if they wished.

By late afternoon, both the children were exhausted. Weet had slowed to a walk and even Sally had ceased her random wanderings. During the increasingly frequent stops, Weet would look around, as if searching for something. When he finally found what he was looking for, he changed direction, heading for a small, rocky hill over to their left. As they rounded it, Weet moved quickly towards a large clump of redwood trees. As they approached, Eric noticed a number of figures among the tree-trunks. He slowed down deliberately to let Weet get ahead and signalled to Rose.

"What's the matter? Why are you letting him go on?" she asked tiredly.

"There's someone in those trees that Weet's heading for," he replied.

Rose looked up. She tilted her head to one side and squinted at the trees. "I hope it's his family, I hope they have some decent food and I hope they have somewhere comfortable to sleep."

Weet was almost at the trees, when a number of figures emerged to greet him and a small, brightly-coloured animal burst from the trees and headed towards him. It was slightly larger than a chicken but looked more like a small ostrich. It ran on two legs, while holding a long, thin tail out for balance. Its head was held upright on top of a thin neck and, except for the head and legs, it was covered with feathers. When it reached Weet, it jumped happily around him. Weet

stretched out the hand that was not carrying the egg and attempted vainly to pat the creature's dancing head.

By now, more figures were standing in front of the trees. Two of them were considerably larger than Weet, perhaps six-and-a-half or even seven feet tall. The rest were either Weet's size or much smaller.

As they gathered around Weet, a chorus of high-pitched whistles reached the hesitant Eric and Rose. When the figures turned toward them, Weet beckoned his friends to come closer.

"Well, here goes," said Eric under his breath. "I hope Mom and Dad are as friendly as Weet."

As they walked forward, Weet stepped out to meet them. Pointing at one of the large figures he said hesitatingly, "he...my...father." Moving his finger to indicate the other tall figure he continued, "he...my...mother." Despite the tension, Rose chuckled and Eric had to dig her in the ribs to be quiet.

Weet moved his arm around to include the five other figures the same height as himself. "Us...sister...brother," he said. Seven smaller figures were scattered through the group, mostly peering out from behind the legs of the larger ones. Several had their odd hands clamped firmly over their noses. Weet indicated them broadly, but seemed at a loss to find a word to describe them. The feathered creature, having detached itself from Weet, was warily circling Sally. "Sinor," whistled Weet, pointing at it.

Eric nodded, in what he hoped was a friendly manner, to the fourteen pairs of staring eyes. "Eric, brother," he said, patting himself on the chest. "Rose, sister," he indicated Rose, "and Sally, dog," he concluded.

Weet spoke to his family in a series of high-pitched whistles which produced a chorus of "Eric, Rose, brother, sister, Sa"y" and "dog" in response.

Eric smiled. Weet's mother stepped forward and cupped her hands the way Weet had done after they had rescued him. Eric attempted to copy the motion. Suddenly, everyone was cupping their hands and crowding around the newcomers. The miniature versions of Weet were particularly taken with Sally, who seemed a bit overwhelmed by it all, but she accepted it willingly, never having been a dog to turn down attention or affection.

When things calmed down, Weet carefully removed the precious egg from the crook of his arm where it had nestled all day. Gently, he handed it to his father. The tall figure looked deeply into the semi-transparent shell and held it up to his ear. He looked at Weet and nodded vigorously. Turning, he led the whole group back into the trees.

The redwoods formed an irregular ring, in places two or three trees wide. In the middle was an open area, in the centre of which a much larger and older redwood leaned at a crazy angle against one side of the ring. Two circles of sleeping mats marked where the youngsters slept and two individual ones the places for the parents. Eric was pleased to see that, in addition to the piles of fruit, there were other foods which looked like roots and some smaller seeds. Maybe the diet here wasn't going to be quite so monotonous as he had first suspected.

Weet walked over to the large central redwood. He extended his arm and turned slowly, indicating the surrounding trees, the piles of food and the sleeping mats.

"Home," he said simply.

CHAPTER 11

The Second Night

With much ushering and chattering, the family arranged itself in a rough circle beside the exposed roots of the redwood. Eric and Rose were seated with much ceremony between Weet's parents and Weet himself. Weet's brothers and sisters formed the rest of the circle. Sally and Sinor had reached an understanding. Sinor was leading the way around the circle, digging grubs and insects out of rotting tree branches with sharp foreclaws. Sally watched the process with interest, but turned up her nose whenever Sinor offered her a wriggling sample of his findings.

Weet's family brought more palatable food and eagerly offered it to Eric and Rose. It was much more varied than the fare they had lived on while they were travelling, but Eric found himself craving something familiar. So did Sally, who quietly slipped away to do some searching on her own. With a backward glance at Weet, Sinor followed.

The wide eyes of the smallest family members never left Eric and Rose. They watched every mouthful as if something wonderful could be learned from it. Eric caused a sensation when he took out his knife and peeled the tough skin off some potato-like root vegetables which tasted surprisingly sweet. Everyone wanted to try, but Weet's parents wouldn't let anyone touch the knife. As Eric's stomach began to fill and the tiredness from the day's travelling began to settle into comfortable relaxation, he took stock of their situation.

He felt safer than he had done on the two previous days. It was extraordinary how quickly he and Rose had adapted to the incredible events. They had no control over what was going on and had hardly had time to think, let alone worry. If they were stuck here, and Eric certainly couldn't see how they were going to get out, then being with Weet and his family wouldn't be too bad.

They lived a very simple life. They had no tools. Their world appeared to provide all that they required to survive. The food would keep Eric and Rose alive, however much Eric might crave hamburgers. Weet was making remarkable progress learning their language. Soon they would really be able to talk and Eric could discover some of the answers to the hundreds of questions that no one in his world had ever been able to ask. Then he might well be famous, if he could only find someone to tell.

There were certainly attractions to this world. Of course, there were dangers too, but here, at least, Eric wasn't a child. No one told him what to do. In fact, in a world without tools, his knife with all its attachments probably made him the most important intelligent being around. The problem was, how long would this world last? They were in the Late Cretaceous, Eric knew that, but how late was it? Things were changing, but how rapidly were they changing and how close were they to the final big bang that ended this idyllic world?

Eric's reverie was interrupted by a distant barking. What kind of trouble had Sally got herself into now? Led by Eric and Rose, everyone worked their way over to the edge of the trees closest to the sound. What they saw there made Eric wish he had brought a camera. In the middle of the open grassy area stood a huge animal that was almost as familiar to Eric as the small brown ball of hair darting around its feet.

The animal was a bull pachyrhinosaurus. It was the size of a large rhinoceros, but differed markedly at both ends. At one end, a long, thick tail stretched back. At the other, a massive head swung from side to side. The front of the head ended in a vast, curved beak which looked like it could cut through small trees with ease. The back of the head flared into a wide, ornamented frill which covered the neck and stretched over the shoulders. The head was topped by a series of horns and knobs in bright shades of green, a contrast to the bluish grey of the body. Every time the animal lowered its head, the frill was magnificently displayed. And, right now, the animal was lowering its head a great deal.

Between the frill and the beak, the animal's head supported a bulging mass of bone. This turned it into a formidable battering ram, capable of discouraging all but the most dangerous predator. Eric imagined the bony head being very effective against a large, relatively slow adversary, but it did have disadvantages against a small agile one. In fact, the pachyrhinosaurus would probably have fared better in a life or death struggle with a tyrannosaurus than it was currently doing against Sally and Sinor. The beast appeared confused as it stumbled from side to side in vain attempts to crush a barking Sally, who was rushing around the increasingly dusty battleground. Sinor kept his distance from the thundering feet, but whenever he saw an opening, he jumped at the animal's sides, even landing briefly on its back.

The cause of the excitement was revealed as the pachyrhinosaurus swung its four-ton bulk around. Huddled under its belly were two babies. About the size of large dogs, they had to crouch to fit under their parent. However, they looked skinny and out of proportion. Their legs were too long and they had not yet developed a neck frill or bony battering-ram. Whether Sally mistook them for a strange form of cat or merely wanted to play, they were obviously the cause of her high spirits. At every opportunity, she would rush in and try to nip one of the babies' flanks. Then she would dance away before father's lumbering legs could squash her. Sinor was not so interested in the babies, but was obviously having fun with his jumping game.

Eric didn't want to see either Sally or the babies hurt by the maddened bull, so he called Sally as loudly as he could. Eventually, the excited dog came panting over. Sinor followed in response to Weet's

whistles. The pachyrhinosaurus first looked as if it were debating pursuit but decided to retreat into some distant trees.

Well, that was one reason Weet considered their circle of trees home. They were close enough together to keep out any large wandering dinosaurs. If a ceratopsian couldn't make it through, then a tyrannosaurus probably couldn't either. Eric felt he would sleep a little more soundly knowing that.

By the time they returned to the central tree, darkness was beginning to fall. Weet spoke rapidly to his brothers and sisters, who disappeared briefly, only to reappear with armfuls of twigs and branches.

"Fire?" asked Weet hopefully, looking at Eric.

"Yeah, let's have a fire." Rose sounded enthusiastic.

"But we've only three matches left." Eric was uncertain.

"So," replied Rose, "what are we saving them for? Do you want to have a dinosaur barbecue?"

Rose was right. With only three matches, there was little point in saving them. If fire were going to be a factor in their new lives, they would have to learn to make it without matches.

"O.K.," said Eric, looking at Weet, "but let's not set it quite so close to the trees."

Soon they had a good-sized blaze going. Weet's family nervously kept well away at first, but when they saw Weet, Eric and Rose settle themselves close to it, they gradually moved closer. In fact, after a while, they pulled the sleeping mats over. Eric had to gently make sure they didn't bring them too close.

When the sleeping mats were arranged in a wide

circle and everyone was stretched with his feet towards the fire, one of Weet's parents built a small nest for the egg within its sleeping mat. Eric thought it was the one that Weet had introduced as his father, but he wasn't sure. Interesting that the father should be the one to incubate the egg. Eric remembered reading that that was what emus did.

Eric chuckled and sneezed.

"What is it?" asked Rose sleepily.

"I was just, *achoo*, thinking how like summer, *achoo*, camp this is," he replied. "All we need is a guitar and a few, *achoo*, rounds of 'Row, Row, Row Your Boat'."

"How many dinosaurs usually go to your summer camp?" said Rose, as she lay back and burrowed into the soft vegetation.

"*Achoo*, not many," said Eric distractedly through a stream of tears and a steadily clogging nose.

"What's the matter with you?" Rose was mumbling now, on the edge of sleep.

"I don't know," replied Eric, "*Achoo*...I must be allergic to something in the sleeping nest." A brief search revealed some tiny yellow flowers attached to the underbrush of Eric's bed.

"It's these little flowers," he informed his sister.

"Well, get rid of them!" Rose sounded less than sympathetic. "Then we can all get some sleep."

Eric picked all the flowers he could find and threw them into the fire. Almost immediately he felt better. Eric looked around the strange circle of faces reflected in the firelight. Despite his allergy attack, he felt oddly relaxed and at ease with this new family. This was the first time he had felt that way since they had arrived.

The thought made him feel guilty as he remembered his distraught parents, searching fruitlessly in the badlands of the other world. They had to get back, but how? Maybe he could persuade some of Weet's brothers and sisters to return with him to the hole by the sea and dig out a new entrance. Maybe then they could crawl back through. But if they could, then so could Weet and his family and what would be the consequences of that? It was all so confusing.

Another thought struck Eric as he lay back beside his sister. If time meant anything at all, tomorrow would be the third day since they had all set off on that Sunday excursion to the badlands of Alberta. Tomorrow would be his twelfth birthday. Suddenly Eric felt very tired and a lot older than his years. He closed his eyes against the flickering firelight.

"Good night, Rose," he whispered, but she was already asleep.

A soft chorus of good nights echoed around the circle.

CHAPTER 12

A Hadrosaur Ride

The next morning, Eric was the first to awaken. It took him a few moments to work out where he was. He hadn't slept well. Despite his tiredness, he had woken up several times and had trouble going back to sleep. First, his knife was digging into his side until he sleepily removed it. Once, he had opened his eyes to see several pairs of tiny red dots peering out of the blackness. As his eyes adjusted to the dull glow of the dying fire, Eric saw that they belonged to small shrew-like creatures about the size of mice. They scattered to the limits of the firelight when he moved to put more wood on the fire.

"Hang in there, guys," he mumbled to them, as he got back into bed. "Your turn will come."

Later, a gentle warm rain woke him briefly. The morning sky was still overcast and filled with heavy clouds. The second night had not been as cold as the one before, but Eric still decided to get up and look for more wood to keep the fire alive. When he stood up, he noticed the knife he had removed in the night. The compass had come loose. Tightening it, he headed for some dead branches of the falling redwood.

He never reached them. A whistle echoed through his head, blurring his vision and making the ground dance under his feet. Instinctively, he turned back towards Rose and caught a glimpse of her writhing in her sleeping mat with her hands over her ears. Then he slumped forward. The last thing he saw before he passed out were two long arms, each ending in three black-clawed fingers, reaching down to pick up his now-still sister. "Rose," he managed to croak before he felt strong arms sliding under his shoulders and the world went black.

For the second time that morning, Eric awoke without knowing where he was. However, he did know that he had a splitting headache, something was digging into his stomach and he was being slowly shaken to pieces. With an effort, he opened his eyes, only to close them again promptly. Ten feet below him the swaying ground sent waves of nausea through his empty stomach. He was on the back of a large animal and the knee he had glimpsed out of the corner of his eye strongly suggested that he wasn't alone.

Very slowly and very carefully, he opened one eye, only to see a wall of brownish-green skin which stretched away to the swaying ground. The knee resembled one of Weet's. Eric craned his head to look around.

Another animal was travelling on a parallel course about fifteen feet away. It was a duckbilled dinosaur

like the parasaurolophus and maiasauras they had seen the day before, but this one had a large, yellow, hatchet-shaped crest sticking straight out from its forehead. It was walking rapidly on its powerful back legs and held its shorter forelegs tucked against its chest. A short, thick tail was held out horizontally and moved up and down to balance the movements of its body as it strode forward.

"Lambeosaurus," thought Eric dully. "This is some introduction to Cretaceous wildlife."

Straps of what looked like creepers on which the nans grew were stretched under the lambeosaurus' belly and around its shoulders. They secured a seat, woven of the same material, above the animal's swaying hips. Other lengths of twine ran forward to a crude harness around the mouth and could obviously be used to pass commands. The creature in the saddle looked like some unearthly cowboy. He was a larger version of Weet and wore a short tunic of yellow and black feathers.

Eric was impressed, both by the casual way the rider controlled his mount and by the fact that the feathers in his suit must at some time have been plucked from a velociraptor.

"Help." Rose's half-angry, half-pleading shout came from the familiar head protruding, like Eric's, from in front of the saddle. "Eric, help."

"I'm over here," Eric shouted back.

"What are they doing with us? Where are we going? What did they do to Weet?"

All of these were very good questions to which Eric didn't have any answers.

"I don't know. Maybe they're taking us to their home." He stopped talking, although his brain continued speculating on reasons for their capture. None that he came up with was particularly reassuring.

Just as he was beginning to really scare himself with some particularly horrible reasons, the lambeosaurs halted at the crest of a small ridge. Craning his neck forward, Eric saw a wide, treeless valley. Barren and uninviting, it was cut by numerous erosion gullies which joined the sluggish river meandering along the valley floor.

On the near slope, a herd of large, four-legged animals was browsing in the short grass and sparse bushes. These creatures were even larger than the pachyrhinosaurus of the previous evening, but instead of the bony mass on the head, each animal sported three long horns. Triceratops, thought Eric, who was beginning to feel that his life was becoming a test on dinosaur recognition. This herd was being patrolled by several of the cowboy dinosaurs mounted on lambeosaurs.

Below them, in a lazy loop of the river, nestled a collection of round huts. They were surrounded by a high wall of woven branches. Thin columns of smoke rose straight into the air from numerous small fires in front of individual huts. Figures stirred in the open areas while several lambeosaurs were tethered together in a corral on the far bank of the river. The air was filled with a strange assortment of grunts and howls. After a brief exchange of whistles between their riders, the mounts began the descent to the village and whatever it held in store.

CHAPTER 13

Fire for the King

A large crowd had gathered by the time Eric and Rose reached the village. It watched in curious silence as the lambeosaurs lurched forward onto their front feet and then down onto their knees to allow the captives to slide off. Eric 's head still hurt and every bone in his body ached. On two shaky legs he stumbled over to Rose, whose grubby cheeks were smeared with tears. As soon as she stood up, she grabbed Eric around the waist and held on tight.

"It's O.K.," he reassured her. "We'll be fine. We're still together." Rose only squeezed harder and buried her face in his chest. "Hey, don't squeeze so hard. I've got enough bruises."

"I'm scared. I want to go home. Why did they bring us here? I want Mommy and Daddy."

This Rose sounded much younger than the one who had barrelled down the beach to rescue Weet two days before. Eric felt both angry and protective. With as much dignity as he could muster with Rose clinging to him, he addressed the crowd.

"What do you want?" The only response was a continuation of the silent stares. At least the creatures didn't look aggressive — or hungry, he thought with a shiver. But how could you read the thoughts behind those expressionless masks?

Apart from height differences and the short, armless tunics of velociraptor feathers that some of them wore, it was impossible to tell them apart. The creatures looked identical to Weet and his family, except that their skin was faintly mottled and their stomachs and arms had a bluish hue. The green skin apparently darkened with age, since the larger individuals were almost black, while the small ones running around their parents' legs were the colour of spring leaves.

Eric had almost decided to try his 'chest-beating/my name is Eric' routine, when the two individuals who had captured them reappeared. Gently but firmly, they pushed the two towards the gap in the fence which marked the gate into the village.

Rose had calmed down a bit, but she kept her arm firmly around his waist and he kept his protectively over her shoulder. As they moved forward, the crowd parted to let them through.

Eric's first impression was that he had entered one of the African villages that his grandmother had described so often. However, this one had been built in a great hurry by someone who was very inexperienced in building. The fence was the most impressive thing about it. Consisting of a solid mass of branches from which protruded vicious-looking thorns, it towered above the huts. Inside the wall, the huts were scattered randomly. Someone had tried, unsuccessfully, to make them circular. Equally unsuccessfully, they had also tried to make the walls vertical.

The huts were constructed of dried mud over crudely interlaced branches which stuck out here and there. There were no windows, although some had vaguely circular holes, suggesting a deliberate attempt to let in light and air.

The protruding branches were draped with nan creepers like those which Eric had noticed on the lambeosaurus' reins. Frequently, these supported bunches of fruit. The hut roofs appeared equally ramshackle, supporting a thatch of leaves, grass and twigs, held in place by an occasional rock.

"They aren't very good builders," Eric pointed out to Rose. "I hope there are no big bad wolves around. This looks like a town built by the two lazy little pigs. One good breath and it would fall down."

Rose smiled at that and Eric felt more secure knowing that their captors were not very good at something. "Maybe no one has ever taught them how to make bricks," she added.

"I wonder why they bother," said Eric, thinking out loud. "Weet's family doesn't seem to build anything..." he paused thoughtfully, "and Weet had never seen fire before, while these people seem to know all about it."

Outside each hut, a small, rough ring of stones enclosed a smouldering pile of branches and twigs, most of which gave off a thin streamer of smoke. On a rock beside each one sat a figure whose job was obviously to tend the fire, although nothing was cooking and heat was certainly not needed at this time of day.

Eric took most of this in as they were led through the village. Eventually, they were ushered into a large open area. The crowd, which had followed them, now formed a large circle with only a small gap in its far side. After a moment, a rustle of anticipation passed through the crowd and the gap widened to admit a group of figures. The group was led by a tall figure that Eric immediately assumed to be the chief, for he was dressed in a full-length tunic of velociraptor feathers. The chief seemed even taller because of a magnificent feather headdress which bobbed regally with each step.

Once in the centre of the circle the group halted before Eric and Rose. Eric was awed, but, after the wonders of the last two days, not especially afraid. Taking the initiative, he patted his chest and said his name three times.

Nothing happened. He repeated the gesture, this time including Rose. At this, the chief stepped forward and launched into a long whistling speech with much arm waving. Eric tried to make out individual sounds, but all he could manage was the sound 'hom', which always seemed to be accompanied by a broad sweeping gesture. At the end of the speech, the chief tilted his befeathered head and regarded Eric.

"It's your turn," whispered Rose.

"Great," Eric whispered back, "but what'll I say?"

"Oh, it doesn't matter," said Rose. "They won't

understand it anyway. Just make it sound important."

Eric thought for a minute. The only thing that came into his mind was the Calgary Flames hockey game his father had taken him to the week before. He took a deep breath and began to sing:

"O Canada,
Our home and native land
True patriot love
In all thy sons' command..."

His voice went squeaky over the second last "O Canada, we stand on guard for thee," but, overall, he felt it went well. He wondered if he had somehow claimed this geological period for Canada and wished he had a flag to dramatically plant in the ground before him. The chief nodded in what Eric hoped was approval. Flushed with his success, Eric stepped forward and cupped his hands in the gesture of welcome that had been so successful when he had met Weet's family.

This was a serious mistake. The chief took a step back and a low whistle passed through the crowd. Obviously, Eric had done something wrong. Whether it had been the gesture or the step forward he couldn't tell but, in either case, it was too late now to repair the damage. Thoughts of the Canadian empire faded as powerful hands gripped Eric's arms and held him firmly in place.

"Brilliant, Eric! Ouch, let go!" It was Rose, swinging from sarcasm to anger. Out of the corner of his eye, Eric saw a small foot connect with a thin greenish shin. A sharp whistle, which Eric took to signify pain, gave him some satisfaction, but too many hands were holding them for any chance of escape.

As soon as the scuffle was over, the chief turned and gestured for a pile of branches to be laid on the ground before Eric. One of his captors removed the knife from Eric's belt and placed it to one side. Pointing from the pile to the knife the chief waved his fingers above the branches.

"They want you to make a fire." Rose was always good at charades.

"O.K.," agreed Eric, "but why? They already have fire."

"I don't know." Rose sounded exasperated. "Just do it. It might make up for your dumb song."

Eric shot Rose a glance to remind her that the song had been partly her idea, but he stepped forward towards the pile of branches. The hold on his arms relaxed enough to allow him to kneel down. Removing the compass from the knife handle, he took out one of the two remaining matches and struck it. The match head disintegrated into small soggy bits which stuck to the roughened knife handle.

"Oh, no!"

"Eric, what's the matter?" Rose sounded worried.

"It's the matches," Eric replied. "The compass came loose when I took the knife off last night. The matches must have got wet in the rain. They won't work. And they were *supposed* to be waterproof."

There was no point in trying the last match now. Perhaps if it dried out it might work. Eric screwed the compass back onto the knife and stood up. He held out the useless match to the chief and shrugged.

"It got wet," he said. "It wasn't supposed to, but

now it doesn't work." He shrugged his shoulders and hoped for the best. The best is not what happened.

After several attempts to convince Eric to light the fire, the chief lost patience. Striding off rapidly through the scattered crowd, he beckoned for Eric and Rose to be brought along. The chief led the way to the far side of the village, where the heavy thorn fence was almost twenty feet high. A rough, circular enclosure was built against the fence. It was the same height as the fence, but tapered gradually to the top, rather like a large chimney. The branches and thorns were so tightly woven together that it was impossible to see through them.

The chief stopped, pointed at the enclosure and whistled instructions to the owner of the hands still holding Eric. Eric found himself shoved towards a hole in the enclosure wall. The sight that met him made Eric wish he could suddenly be transported back into Mr. Smith's math class. In the centre of the enclosure squatted a velociraptor, staring dully at the wall in front of it. The bones of its narrow head stuck out and its belly was sunken and hollow. It looked as if it hadn't had anything to eat for a long time.

As Eric watched, the beast blinked and raised its clawed foot to scratch gently at the back of its head. Then it yawned and turned to look straight at Eric. For a moment, their eyes were locked and Eric had the uncomfortable feeling that the creature was trying to hypnotize him. Then it leaped. In silence and without any sign of preparation, it cleared the six feet separating it from its prey and crashed into the fence. If the guard had not been so quick in pulling Eric back, the flashing claw would not have missed its target and the velociraptor would no longer have been quite so hungry.

Eric gulped. He was glad the guard was holding him, because he didn't trust his legs. From the crashes on the other side of the fence, the velociraptor continued to hurl itself at the branches, which shook but seemed to be strong enough.

"What is it? What's in there?" Rose sounded as if she didn't really want to know the answer to her questions.

Eric answered anyway.

"It's a velociraptor," he said, "a very hungry one."

CHAPTER 14

Survival of the Fittest

Both the children thought of the starving velociraptor as they were led in silence back to the central clearing. There, the chief went through his 'make a fire' charade and Eric repeated his explanation about the wet matches. With an imagination fuelled by the creature in the enclosure, Eric added a pantomime that involved pointing at the last match and at the sun which was beginning to break through the clouds. He had not much hope that he could convey the concept of drying the match, but he hoped that his gestures might indicate a mystical link between the sun and the match.

After several repetitions of this pantomime, the chief seemed to get the point. He whistled commands to the guards and strode away. Much to their relief, Eric and Rose were led in the opposite direction from the velociraptor to a hut with no fire outside. The last match was taken from Eric and placed almost reverently on a flat smooth stone in the middle of a patch of sunlight. The pair was then ushered into the hut.

Inside, the hut was bare and dingy, although a fair amount of light filtered through the door, walls and roof. The floor was made of hard-packed earth and there was no furniture. The more-or-less flat roof only just allowed Eric to stand up. No one followed them in, but, through the opening, Eric could see the legs of a guard.

Eric sat down disconsolately. It was a bleak sort of prison. He wished he were back in the friendly tree-circle home of Weet and his family. The match, which had once promised so much in this world, was now the only thing standing between Eric and Rose and a grisly end in the velociraptor enclosure.

"Want to know something funny?" Eric turned to his sister. "I won't be born for millions of years, and today is my twelfth birthday. I thought I was going to be old, but I never guessed how old I really was."

Rose put her arm around her brother.

"Happy Birthday," she said with a smile. Then she burst out laughing. "Do you know what I got you for a present?"

"No," replied Eric, "you didn't put it with Mom and Dad's presents in the closet."

"I know you look in there and I wanted it to be a surprise," Rose managed through her laughter. "I bought you a book on dinosaurs. The big one you liked at the museum. Mom gave me the money."

Eric was laughing now too. "You mean the one with all the pictures of what different artists thought it

was like when the dinosaurs were alive?"

The two children hugged each other hard to stop the laughter spilling over into tears. Gradually, they lapsed into silence. It was broken by Rose, voicing a thought that had been in both their minds.

"They wouldn't really feed us to that thing, would they?"

"I don't know." Eric was tired. "Let's hope the match dries out. Then, at least, we can light his majesty one fire. Maybe that'll keep him happy. It sure won't do him any good to threaten us with the velociraptor when there are no matches left. But why is he so desperate for us to light him a fire and how did he know we had matches in the first place?"

Suddenly Eric remembered the feeling he had had while they were travelling yesterday.

"They followed us. All yesterday I felt we were being watched. I thought it was just because everything was so weird, but we really were being watched. They followed us all day. They probably saw us light the fire last night and maybe even the one in the morning. But why?"

"Oh, Eric. You always have to have a reason for everything." Rose sounded exhausted. "What does it matter why? Maybe they just wanted to be able to light fireworks safely."

"Yeah," he admitted, laughing, "maybe they just liked the idea of matches." A thought began to form in his mind. "Or maybe they really can't make fire."

"Of course they can, Eric. There must be a hundred fires in the village. There's one outside every hut."

"Exactly." Eric couldn't help asking a question.

"Why? They're not cooking anything. It's warm today. It was even quite warm last night. They don't need those fires, so why is someone tending every single fire? Unless they can't make fire themselves and have to be sure the ones they have don't go out."

"But how did they get fire in the first place if they can't make it?" Rose responded to the questions despite herself.

"Lightning strikes." Eric was on a roll. "Brush fires must be pretty common here whenever there's a storm. When the nights first got cold, someone must have had the idea of trapping fire to keep warm. It was probably easy enough to collect a smoking branch and start a fire with it. That was probably the first step. Then, they had the problem of keeping the fire going. I guess a larger group would have an advantage since lots of fires are not likely to go out all at once. That was the beginning of villages."

Eric began to think of other things he had seen.

"They're not used to living close together, so they built huts, not very good ones, but enough for privacy and probably to keep in the heat on a cold night. But once they started living in groups, they became an attractive food source for predators, so they built a wall to keep them out."

"But what about the dinosaurs they ride?" Rose asked. "Why did they start using them?"

Eric thought for a minute. "Maybe they used them before, or perhaps this has been going on for long enough for them to train or breed the lambeosaurs. When they started settling down and living in villages, they would have eaten all the surrounding food pretty quickly. Look at how barren this valley is. Then, either they would have to grow their own food, or find a way to look for food over a much wider area. That's probably what they use the lambeosaurs for, food gathering."

The mention of food triggered another thought in Eric's racing brain.

"The triceratops!"

"The what?" asked Rose.

"The triceratops," Eric repeated. "The herd we saw on the way in. They're too slow for food gathering and I didn't see any signs of agriculture. I doubt they're used for pulling anything. I wonder if they're being kept for food."

"But Weet only eats fruit," interrupted Rose.

"I know," continued Eric, "but here things are different. Maybe the villagers are trying to get more food by turning to meat eating. Or maybe the meat is for the velociraptors. They seem to like them. The chief was wearing enough of their feathers and we know they have at least one in a cage. And a pack of trained velociraptors would sure be a great way to control everyone."

Eric didn't particularly like the direction of his thoughts. The image of an unscrupulous chief with a dozen trained velociraptors was hardly comforting.

"Anyway, this is all just guesswork. The only thing we know for sure is that these guys are very imaginative. They're in the middle of developing a new way of life because of the changes in the climate."

Rose was impressed.

"You worked all that out?" she asked.

Eric was tempted to take credit.

"Well, some of it," he said modestly, "but most of it I remember from a book I read on early man. It was about how the Neanderthals couldn't adapt during the last ice age and our ancestors could. So our ancestors survived and the Neanderthals died out."

"Does that mean that Weet's people are going to die out?"

Eric looked at Rose in surprise. He hadn't made that connection.

"I don't know," he said slowly. "Well, they don't seem to be able to adapt as well as this lot does. They're still living a life suited to an earlier Cretaceous climate, when nature provided everything they needed.

Eric was confused again, not by the facts, but by his own feelings. Despite the fact that their present captors threatened to feed them to his worst nightmare, he had a grudging respect for them. They were doers. They were meeting their changing world head on and trying to come to terms with it. But the price they were paying was high. Eric imagined that even the position of chief was a result of needing someone in charge in the midst of change. All this somehow made them seem very human.

Eric's mind returned to the previous evening. He remembered the easy-going friendship he had felt with Weet and his family. He remembered how comfortable and secure he had felt, the only time he had felt that way since their arrival. Was it worth giving up all that for the sake of warmth?

"You know," he said, "these guys probably lived the

same kind of life as Weet. No worries. They didn't need to plan for the future, they didn't need to build shoddy, little huts to live in and huge fences to keep themselves safe. They didn't need a chief dressed up in feathers. I wonder if any of them regret giving up their freedom in exchange for a little warmth? The funny part is that it doesn't matter either way. This whole world is doomed and all the Weets and all the chiefs with it."

Eric lay back on the earthen floor. He felt like crying. This wasn't like his dream world. That world was simple and straightforward. In reality, this world was just as complicated and difficult as his own. At least with math...

Suddenly, Eric noticed that the ground was shaking. Very gently, but it was shaking. But that was not what had interrupted his reverie. Very faintly, and from very far away, Eric heard a dog bark.

CHAPTER 15

Rescue

Eric sat up. The shaking was still gentle, but now it was accompanied by a distant rumble, like a faraway train. His first thought was "earthquake," but what would Sally have to do with an earthquake?

"What's that noise?" Rose looked around worriedly.

"I don't know," Eric replied as he crawled towards the doorway. Very carefully, he stuck his head out. All around, figures were crawling out of huts. Even their guard had taken a few steps aside and was looking off in the distance. Eric took a chance, crawled outside and stood up. The noise was much louder now and he could see a cloud of dust boiling up into the sky. Video recreations of Indian buffalo jumps sprang into his mind.

"Stampede!"

Rose stuck her head out of the hut door. "What's happening?"

Figures were beginning to move away from the

cloud and the noise. Some were running.

"Its a stampede," Eric had to shout. He helped Rose out. Everyone was running now. Their guard was nowhere to be seen.

"I wonder if the thorn fence will hold?"

Almost at once, Eric's question was answered. From around the hut in front of them lumbered a confused triceratops. Swinging its head from side to side, it stumbled against the hut, which promptly disintegrated into a pile of branches and mud. A piece of brush from the roof landed in the fire, causing it to flare up in a column of sparks and flame. The triceratops shied violently away, destroying the adjoining hut and bumping another frightened beast. Either the thorn fence had given way, or these scattered animals had found their way through the gateway. In any case, it would not be long before the rest of the panicked herd followed them.

A low bellow made Eric turn to see a third triceratops threading its way between the huts. He bent to pick up the match from the rock beside the door and then reached up to yank a branch out of the hut roof.

"I hope you're dry," he said and struck the match on the handle of his knife. Nothing happened. Another triceratops moved towards them.

"ERIC!" Rose yelled frantically.

Eric closed his eyes while he struck the match again. With a low hiss, it spluttered into life.

"I hope you're dry," he repeated and held the match to the end of the branch. With a reassuring crackle, the twigs flared up. Eric waved the branch at the approaching animal which swerved away and disappeared between the remains of the huts. But more triceratops were appearing all the time. They hesitated when they saw the fire in Eric's hand, but they were beginning to jostle each other. Soon the pressure from behind would force them forward and then one flaming branch wouldn't stop them. Eric touched his branch to the tinder-dry roof and the hut burst into flames.

"Let's go," he said and led the way towards the centre of the village.

The central area was in total confusion. Figures milled everywhere and, here and there, a frightened triceratops stumbled dangerously about. At first, Eric thought of setting fire to the circle of huts to keep the stampede out, but it was too late for that. Every second, more triceratops were entering the compound. Eric picked the side where there seemed to be fewest and, leading Rose with one hand and frantically waving his flaming branch in the other, struggled through the chaos.

Once among the huts again it was easier to move. The children soon found themselves standing beneath the thorn fence which was still intact, except for a large, ragged hole, probably made by one of the stampeding animals.

"There's our way out," said Eric, making for the hole.

He had to move carefully, because the ground was littered with broken branches with inch-long, curved thorns. They seemed to be almost alive as they continually snagged his trouser legs. To keep his balance and leave both hands free to unsnag his trousers, he threw what was left of his burning branch through the hole onto the dry ground outside.

Rose was having an even harder time.

"Eric, wait."

In his rush to escape, Eric had gone several steps ahead of Rose. Now he turned to find her no-longer white trousers firmly snagged on a large branch in the thorn wall.

"Hold on, don't struggle." Eric worked his way towards her. He was too slow. Balancing on her left leg, Rose had managed to pull the right one free, but the sudden jerk had pushed her backwards. By the time Eric reached her, she was firmly attached to the thorn wall.

"O.K., hold still," he said as he began the laborious process of freeing his sister. He was about half done, when he heard Rose gasp. Looking around, he saw a huge triceratops standing no more than ten feet away. It was the largest Eric had seen that day. Had he been standing beside it, (which he had no desire to do), the curve of the beast's back would have been well above his head. The neck frill was richly ornamented and colourful, while above each eye grew a wicked, four-foot-long horn which, when the animal's head was lowered as it was now, pointed straight at Eric.

The triceratops was upset. It pawed the ground, as it tried to decide what to do. Eric could see no way to help it make up its mind. His fiery branch was out of reach and shouting might just antagonize the animal more. Very slowly, he continued freeing Rose's clothes from the thorns. A point exactly between his shoulder blades itched uncontrollably as he thought of the horns pointing directly at it.

Eric had almost convinced himself that he would succeed and that he and Rose could slip away, when he heard a loud snort. The triceratops had lowered its head even farther. As it did so, it was backing away and pawing the ground heavily. It looked as if it had finally made up its mind to impale these annoying little creatures on its impressive horns. All it needed was a little more space for the run up.

Eric's hands were sweating and slippery as he tore at the remaining thorns. Rose was whimpering quietly. Behind him, the snorting continued. He mustn't look back. Only a few more. He would make it, he would make it.

No, he wouldn't.

The triceratops charged. Eric ripped frantically at the last few thorns, encouraged by the thundering hooves behind him.

Rose screamed.

So did the triceratops.

Eric turned to see the animal lurching sideways. Clinging to its side was the starving velociraptor. Its forefeet held onto the much larger animal's back where its ravenous jaws were taking tearing bites. The claws on its hind feet were embedded in the triceratops' flanks.

Still screaming, the triceratops with its bizarre burden lurched off down the open space between the thorn wall and the nearest huts. Eric almost fainted. His heart was still racing and his lungs didn't seem able to pull in enough air. With shaking hands, he

unhooked the final thorn and pulled Rose away from the wall. In silence, the pair picked their way through the hole and collapsed panting on the ground.

The hom's whistling that morning had only knocked Weet out for a few moments, but it had been time enough for them to spirit Eric and Rose away. He came around to the sound of Sally barking frantically at the edge of the trees. The rest of his family was sitting or standing about looking stunned. The homs must have followed them back. Perhaps it was even the two he had seen on his walkabout.

Groggily, Weet crawled to the edge of the trees. Sally and Sinor were running about in the clearing. Sally would run off barking to the next clump of trees, then she would turn and come tearing back to run in circles around Sinor, trying to get him to follow her. Sinor appeared undecided and kept looking back at the trees. By now, several of Weet's age-mates and a few of the hatchlings had joined him.

Weet didn't think twice. He had to try to rescue Eric and Rose. His family knew that he and Eric and Rose were bound together by the events of the walkabout. They understood. With only a brief goodbye to the age-mates closest to him, Weet walked out of the trees.

As soon as Sinor saw Weet coming towards him, he took off after Sally. There was no way he was going to be left out of this adventure.

Sally and Sinor led the way. They would rush ahead,

following the homs' trail. Every so often, Sally would rush back to show Weet the way and encourage him to greater speed. Not that Weet needed to be shown the way. He was pretty sure the homs were heading for the village by the river. It was their closest community, but he did wonder why they had kidnapped his new friends. Weet's family and the homs didn't like each other, but, until now, they had carefully avoided any contact.

Often Weet had watched the hom village from the ridge above. It seemed like a very strange way to live, all cramped together with no trees around them, but he did admire many of their abilities — riding the shovelbills, for instance. That had been the reason behind his persuading his father to try raising a shovelbill from an egg and why his walkabout task had been to collect that egg. He had hoped that the egg might change their lives, but he had not suspected how dramatically.

Half-way through the day, Weet began to recognize his surroundings as being close to the hom village. Whistling softly, he called Sinor to him. Sally followed close behind. Slowly, the unlikely trio crept up the ridge and peered over. There was the village all right, but, if his friends were in it, how was he going to get them out? He had not thought that far ahead. When he spotted the herd of horned crestnecks, an idea began to form.

That idea sprang from his watching Sally and Sinor with the crestneck the day before. If these creatures reacted the same way, he might be able to start them towards the village to cause confusion. During the panic, he might be able to find Eric and Rose and escape.

He knew it wasn't a very good idea, but he couldn't think of anything better. In fact, his idea turned out to be almost too good. The instant Sally and Sinor burst from the trees, the crestnecks panicked. The whistles of the few mounted homs were too late and were lost in the thunder of hooves, as the massive beasts rushed down the hillside. Looking ridiculously small to be the cause of such a movement, Sally and Sinor charged after the herd, nipping and jumping at any animals who were slowing down.

The herd charged down the slope and, before it could swerve, found itself funnelled by the river banks into the loop where the village lay. The lead animals tried to veer around the thorn walls, but the ones behind were going too fast. For a while the wall held and only a few animals found their way in through the gate, but the pressure was too great, and soon whole sections of the wall collapsed.

What followed seemed to Weet like a nightmare. He ran down the hill after the stampeding herd, but with no hope of catching up or of altering events even if he did. All he could do was watch as the terrified crestnecks milled about, destroying the village. In addition to the damage they were doing, thick smoke was now rising as fire took hold of the ruined huts. Homs were escaping through the fence wherever they could and splashing in panic across the river.

Weet felt terrible. Not only had he not meant to destroy the village but, if Eric and Rose were in there, he might have killed them. The situation was getting increasingly out of hand. Weet had the uncomfortable impression that he was struggling against forces far beyond his control. He could no longer see Sinor or Sally. In despair, he sat down on the dusty slope to think about what to do next.

Before he could come to any conclusion, he saw Sally tearing around the side of the village where the wall was least damaged. As soon as she saw Weet, Sally came panting up the hill towards him. Sinor followed close behind. At least, he hadn't lost them.

Just as Sally and Sinor were playfully licking and jumping at him, Weet looked up and saw a sight that made him catch his breath. Around the side of the wall staggered two figures. Each seemed to be propping up the other. They were filthy and their second skins were all torn, but they were recognizably Eric and Rose.

CHAPTER 16

The Hatching

Eric's exhaustion vanished the moment he saw Sally come bounding around the curve of the thorn fence.

"Sally!" he cried happily, as he scratched the panting dog's ear. "Did you do all this?"

Sally wagged her tail even harder. Sinor had followed her round the corner, but he held back from the happy reunion.

"Come on." Eric held out his hand encouragingly. Sinor loped slowly forward and sniffed it. Very gently, Eric moved his hand to ruffle the feathers on the back of Sinor's neck. Sinor tilted his head and regarded Eric lovingly through half-closed eyes.

"We'd better go." It was Rose and she was right. Parts of the village were now burning fiercely and it might be wise to be gone when the homs reorganized and began looking for someone to blame.

"Yeah, you're right." Eric let go of Sinor and rose to his feet. Sally and Sinor bounded away around the wall and Eric and Rose followed wearily. Their spirits picked up and they forgot their aches when they turned the corner and saw Weet sitting on the hillside. The joyful reunion was brief, since everyone was now eager to climb back to the security of the treed ridge.

Once safely among the cool foliage, they turned to survey the scene.

"Wow!" was all Eric could say as he got his first overview of the devastation. "I thought this place was a mess this morning."

Most of the fires in the village had burned out, but columns of hazy smoke still spiralled up from the ruins. About a third of the thorn fence was destroyed and there were ragged holes in the rest. A few triceratops moved aimlessly about on the near bank of the river, but the majority were clustered in small groups on the far side. Scattered among them were individual lambeosaurs which had escaped from the corral. The homs had collected in a loose group on the far river bank, and Eric thought he could see the headdress plumes of their chief near the centre. The velociraptor which had saved their lives was nowhere to be seen. Eric found himself wishing it well in its unequal battle with the triceratops.

"I hope the homs have enough of their village left to keep them warm and protect them tonight," murmured Rose.

"I'm sure they will," replied Eric, surprised by his sister's kind thought. "They're pretty resourceful. It won't take them long to recover, but it might be a while before they try to tame a triceratops herd. Or steal fire again."

"Home. Night." Weet interrupted their conversation by pointing to the sun midway through its afternoon arc. He was fascinated by the scene below and very much wanted to see how the homs would rebuild their village. But it was getting late and they had to go if they were to get back before the dark.

"I guess we'd better get going," agreed Eric. "I hope it's not cold tonight. There're no matches left."

The journey home was uneventful, which was exactly the way Eric wanted it. They arrived back at the tree home just before dusk. This time there was no hesitation and they all passed through the trees together to be welcomed by Weet's family and a much-needed meal of fruit.

After they had eaten, Weet went over to look at the egg. It was ready. When he put it to his ear he could hear the baby's tiny whistles. He handed the egg over to his father. He would hatch it, just as he had done Weet and as Weet had seen him do the hatchlings. Weet's father took the egg, listened for a minute and then gazed thoughtfully into the translucent shell. Slowly, he handed it back to Weet and nodded.

Weet was overcome. He was going to be allowed to hatch it. The job that was usually done by the oldest male in the family was being given to him. He felt as tall as the surrounding trees.

Very slowly, Weet sat down with his legs spread on either side of the makeshift nest. He placed the egg in the nest so that it lay between his knees. With a final look at his father and the circle of watching eyes, he brought his foot up and, with the tiny heel claw, gently pierced the egg. A trickle of clear liquid ran

down the shell. Holding his foot as still as possible, Weet carefully rotated the egg with his hands until he had cut completely around. Slowly, he removed the severed cap and laid the egg on its side in the nest.

Nothing moved. The watchers seemed to be holding their breath. Weet could see the curved back of the baby bulging pale and green out of the hole he had cut. He hoped he had made the hole big enough. All at once, the egg began to move. With a series of convulsive jerks, it rolled around the nest, occasionally bumping into Weet's legs. The bulging back got bigger with each jerk. Suddenly, with an almost audible pop, the back end of the baby was out. With a few more shakes, the rest of the body was free. The baby was wet and glistening in the fading light as it sat confused in the centre of the circle.

"It's hatched," cried Rose. "Oh, isn't it cute?"

To Eric, it looked more ridiculous than cute. It was surprisingly big, considering the size of the egg that had contained it, but most of that size was taken up with skinny legs and an oversized head, from which two wide eyes regarded its audience suspiciously. Weet peeled off a strip of nan and held it out. Hesitatingly, the baby stretched out its scrawny neck and took the offering.

"Oh, can I?" asked Rose. Weet handed her the nan.

As his sister mothered the odd baby, Eric wondered about the future. The baby was the beginning of more than just a single new life. It might be the start of a completely new way of life for all of Weet's people. If the baby survived, and it certainly looked healthy enough right now, Weet's family might have a hadrosaur to ride in a few years. With Eric's help, and, as the homs had proved, even without it, they might have fire by that time too. If the homs left them alone, they would have a new way of life and all that went with it.

But would that be good? There must be other family groups scattered about. Perhaps, in a few generations, they would be living in the same squalor as the homs and would have given up their precious freedom to some chief with feathers on his head. And for what? Their world was doomed, whatever they did. Maybe it would be best to just keep going the way they had for thousands, perhaps millions, of years. But how could Eric make Weet understand that?

As he watched Rose feed the baby, Weet was thinking much the same. Until the dramatic events of today, he had been sure that he wanted to acquire the skills and possessions of the homs who seemed to be able to mould the world around them to their needs. But two events had placed doubts in his mind.

Firstly, he had seen the hom village up close and it had not met his expectations. From his vantage point on the ridge, he had pictured it as well organized, cleverly built and clean; a bustling happy place. From up close, even the undamaged huts had looked squalid and dirty. He doubted that he could ever adapt to living like that.

Secondly, he had seen how easily disaster could

strike the village. The panicked homs, flooding across the river, had been a shock to him. That could never happen to his family. Their group was small enough to scatter and disappear when danger threatened. Even if something destroyed their tree-circle home, it would be easy to find another one. Maybe copying the homs was not as simple as he had thought. This would require some serious thought.

Weet never got a chance to do that serious thinking. A deep roar froze everyone in place.

A shiver passed all the way down Eric's back. Instinctively, Eric knew there was only one creature in this world, or any other, that could make a noise like that: Tyrannosaurus rex.

CHAPTER 17

Escape

The baby was instantly forgotten as everyone crowded to the edge of the trees. In the centre of the clearing, a tyrannosaurus stood silhouetted against the deep orange evening sky. It faced the trees with its head cocked to one side as if listening. Eric tried very hard to give it nothing to hear.

Unlike the velociraptors, it was featherless and had a reddish brown skin crossed by thick black tiger stripes. Despite the lack of feathers, it was still very bird-like. The bulging muscles of the hind legs looked like immense drumsticks. The small forelegs waved about helplessly as the tiny clawed hands jerked open and closed.

But what overawed all the watchers most was the incredible head. It was balanced more than twenty feet in the air and was longer than Eric was tall. Most of that length seemed to be jaws. The beast was slowly opening and closing its mouth, as if to taste the air, and the six-inch long teeth made a horrible clacking sound every time they came together.

As they watched, the beast threw back its head and roared. Of all the incredible sights Eric and Rose had seen, this was the most impressive. Sally and Sinor cowered in the underbrush, all thoughts of teasing long gone.

Eric looked around at his companions. No one made a sound. Eric's brow furrowed with worry. If the beast attacked, would Weet's whistling turn it away? He hoped he would never find out.

Weet lay in the underbrush beside Eric. He hadn't seen many roarers, but this was easily the largest. His father's stillness suggested that he too was overcome by its size. Whistling would only annoy this beast and even the tree ring might not save them. Their best chance was to keep silent and still, in the hope that it would lose interest and leave. Weet hoped that, for once, Eric, Rose and Sally had the sense to do the same.

"Eric," Rose whispered but Eric could feel the tension in the air increase at the sound.

"Shh," he whispered as his nose began to twitch.

The tyrannosaurus cocked its head further round and stopped clacking its teeth.

Rose nudged her brother and pointed to the ground in front of his face. Irritated, Eric looked down, and his eyes widened in horror. Nestled in the twigs was a cluster of tiny yellow flowers.

"Oh no," he gasped as the tickle in his nostrils became unbearable.

"Eric, don't," Rose's whisper was urgent.

The tyrannosaurus took a step in their direction. Eric pinched his nose as hard as he could. It hurt, but it couldn't stop the... *"Achoo!"*

Eric's sneeze sounded like a cannon going off. For one eternal moment, nothing happened. No-one moved. Then the tyrannosaurus roared again. Then it charged. Eric had a glimpse of the huge, bulging muscles of its legs, as they powered the creature's eight-ton bulk towards him. Then he grabbed Rose's arm and hauled her back into the centre of the tree ring.

Everyone else had had the same idea. They were huddled by the base of the tilted redwood when the tyrannosaurus attacked. Incredibly, it didn't even slow down when it came to the trees. It apparently aimed for a gap between the tree supporting the tilted tree and the one next to it. But it miscalculated. The gap was too small. The head fitted through easily, but the huge body stuck at the shoulders. There was a deafening sound of splintering wood and the old tree shuddered violently.

The tyrannosaurus roared. By throwing its bulk from side to side, it pushed farther into the central clearing. A few more thrusts and it would be through. Already, Weet's family had retreated to the back of the clearing. One more push and the massive beast would be upon them.

Weet was in an agony of indecision. Now each of the older family members should grab one of the hatchlings and make an escape through the back of the ring. Once they were dispersed, the roarer would have great difficulty finding them. But his friends seemed incapable of movement and huddled at the base of the centre tree. Any second now, the trees would give way and the roarer would be through. If they didn't act quickly, they were finished.

The roaring and crashing were overpowering Eric's ability to think and act. Not that there was much he could do. Rose was whimpering beside him and Sally was lying flat, as if wishing the ground would swallow her.

If that is what she was wishing in her canine mind, her wish was granted. As the tyrannosaurus made a final lunge, the ground around Eric heaved and the old redwood fell. Huge, gnarled roots rose from the soil, forming a muddy cage around Eric and Rose, cutting off their escape. Under the trunk, a large black hole formed.

Eric could feel the warm breath of those immense jaws. The smell made his stomach heave. Teeth larger than his head tore at the roots in front of him. Behind them, a cavernous throat almost seemed to beckon.

"It won't even need to swallow," was all Eric could think of as he struggled to get as far away as possible.

Rose seemed paralyzed with fear. The old tree was still falling which caused more roots to emerge between the children and the dinosaur. The hole beneath the tree grew bigger.

As the roarer burst into the clearing, Weet's family melted through the back of the circle. Only Weet and Sinor hesitated.

"Eric!" Weet's shout was drowned by the sound of crashing trees and thundering footsteps. The roots of the falling redwood were trapping Eric and Rose.

As the roarer lowered its head towards the exposed roots, Weet leaped into the clearing. Taking a deep breath, he whistled as loudly as he had ever done. Nothing happened. Weet ran forward. The roarer's head was almost resting on the ground and still Weet had to look up to see its enraged red eye. Sinor darted in and jumped at the beast's flanks, but it paid no attention. Weet took another deep breath and whistled.

This time the tyrannosaurus stopped biting at the roots and began to shake its head, as if an annoying insect were buzzing about. Weet kept whistling. The tyrannosaurus raised its head. Now its whole body was swaying from side-to-side. It swung back and forth over Weet's head like a dark, threatening thunder cloud. Weet whistled for all he was worth.

Weet could see Eric and Sally among the roots. They were standing on the edge of a large black hole and were covered by the dirt falling from the roots. Eric had one hand up to his temple and was holding onto Rose with the other. Sally lay beside them. Weet couldn't keep whistling much longer and there was no way Eric could drag everyone out from the clinging roots.

The tyrannosaurus roared again. In obvious pain it lunged against the falling tree. As the rest of the roots ripped out, the ground under Sally gave way. In a scrabbling of claws, she disappeared from sight.

"Sally!" Eric screamed as a large root caught him across the chest. He fell sideways, pushing Rose into the yawning hole below him. Weet watched, horrified, as both his friends disappeared into the inky blackness after their dog. The last echoes of his whistle died between his teeth as the roarer swung back and down. The side of its huge head hit Weet's shoulder a glancing blow, enough to send him completely across the clearing into the ring of trees. Weet felt a sharp pain at the back of his head before blackness descended around him too.

CHAPTER 18

Fame

The earthy blackness was like a long tunnel which Eric was clawing his way through. He couldn't feel or see anything. It was like being lost in a mountain of black cotton wool. Was he suffocating in the earth beneath the tree? Was this what dying was like?

Sensation returned in the form of a sharp pain in his side.

"Come on, wake up, we're there." Rose poked him again, even harder. "It was you who wanted to come. Don't go to sleep."

Eric struggled back with an overpowering sense of confusion. The car was just pulling into a parking lot on the edge of the valley. Behind him, the hoodoos rose, strange and inviting.

"Where are we?" he asked groggily.

"At your stupid dinosaur place, of course." Patience and understanding were not Rose's strong points. "Come on, wake up."

Eric's mind was racing. Not a dream, surely not. It

had been so vivid, so real. An overwhelming sadness flooded over him — Weet, Sinor, the homs, the tyrannosaurus, all the strange and wonderful things that had happened in the last three days. How could it have been only a dream?

"What about Weet? Don't you remember?"

"What are you talking about? Who's Tweet?" Rose was looking at him strangely. Her white trousers were clean and not torn by the homs' thorn fence. With a sense of rising panic, Eric grabbed his knife and unscrewed the compass. Five matches lay dry and unlit inside the handle. Eric sank back in the seat with a sigh.

"No, it's Weet. Never mind." It had just been a dream, after all.

"Mom, Eric's imagining things."

"Stop bickering, you two. We'll be out of the car in a minute." Their father sounded tired.

The family crossed the road and found a quiet, sheltered spot to claim as their own. Eric's thoughts were miles, or millions of years, away as he wandered off to search the ground on the small tributary valley running up towards the cliffs. Sally was already well on her way with her canine explorations.

"Don't go too far and keep an eye on Rose," his mother was shouting after him. "We'll have lunch in about an hour."

Eric didn't go far, just behind a couple of hoodoos. There he sat down, oblivious to Rose and her drawings or Sally and her scratchings. He still couldn't believe it had been just a dream. He could picture everything. He could still feel a tingle of fear at the thought of the tyrannosaurus' jaws about to close on him. He could still smell the alien smells of the world he had visited. He felt close to tears when he thought of Weet's kindly, intelligent eyes and his comical mimicry. Had he and his family escaped from the tyrannosaurus? Did they save the baby? Did they learn to use fire? How could it have been something as simple as a dream?

"Sally's gone in a hole." Eric's skin turned cold, despite the warm sun. Stumbling on the uneven ground, he rushed over to the cleft where Rose was standing. He fully expected to see a round black hole, but there was only an overhang, into whose shade Sally was trying to push her overheated body.

"She's all right," he said. "She's just hot." Then a thought struck him.

"Rose," he continued, "what did you get me for my birthday?"

Rose looked up. "I'm not telling."

"Rose, you've got to. It's important."

"No." Rose sounded adamant. She was enjoying the power over her brother. "It's a surprise. Only mom knows."

Eric sighed with frustration. "Rose, please. This is much more important than a surprise." Eric spoke slowly. "Did you get me that big book with all the pictures of the dinosaurs in it?"

Rose's eyes widened in wonder. "How did you know that?" she asked. "I never thought you'd guess. It was so expensive. Mom gave me the money."

Eric sat back. "I didn't guess, Rose. You told me."

"I never did." Rose was getting defensive.

"Never mind," said Eric quickly. "Rose, don't you remember anything about our adventure?"

A puzzled frown crossed her face. "I..." she began hesitantly.

"What?" asked Eric, leaning forward eagerly.

"There was a monster," she continued, "a really scary monster." Eric was holding his breath. "It had blue hair and green teeth and it chased us down a hole where we met a genie and a beautiful princess." Rose burst out laughing. "Tricked ya, tricked ya, Sally's got to kiss ya."

Eric sighed. He didn't know what was happening. Everything was so confusing. He turned back dejectedly. Something sticking out of the side of the bank above his head caught his eye. He clambered up the slope for a closer look. It was bone all right. As he scraped off more and more of the dirt, his heart leapt with the excitement of recognition. It was a hadrosaur skull.

Only about a third of the head was uncovered, but that was enough. He could see the line of flat teeth, the empty eye socket and the short, stubby crest. Even more exciting were the tips of four vertebrae which formed a line behind the head and disappeared into the rock. This was a complete skeleton, he knew it. This was what he had always wanted, the find which would make him famous. Tentatively, he reached out a hand to stroke the dull crest that he knew had once been a lively red.

"Maiasaura," he muttered, "did Weet ever learn to ride you?" But there was no reply. The skull was cold and lifeless. Just rock and mineral. Nothing remained

of the vibrant world he had witnessed so recently. His eyes began to fill with tears.

"Look, a shooting star!" It was Rose down below him. He looked at the sky over the valley. Arcing across the horizon was a bright band of light streaming behind a fiery head. It was a big meteorite all right, bright enough to be seen in daylight, but it didn't brighten up the world like a flash photograph. One meteorite this size wasn't going to destroy the world. It vanished behind the far wall of the valley.

Eric turned back to his find. This time he noticed something else. Nestled beside the skull was a small collection of fragile-looking bones. With great care, Eric brushed the loose dust and stones off them. He recognized a pattern. There was a confused collection of very small bones. At one end, longer ones were arranged in radiating rows. Sadness overwhelmed him. He sat back and began to cry. Through his tears, he could make out the wavering form of the three long, delicate fingers outlined against the brown rock. This find would definitely make him famous.

THE END

THE WAY NORTH AMERICA LOOKED IN WEET'S TIME

WEET'S WORLD

Weet's world is the Late Cretaceous of Southern Alberta, about 65 million years ago. The fossil remains of many of the familiar animals which shared Weet's world (triceratops, tyrannosaurus, parasaurolophus) are common in the badlands around Drumheller and at Dinosaur Provincial Park near Brooks. Although the rocks at these two locations are separated in time by about ten million years (65 million-year-old Horseshoe Canyon Formation at Drumheller, 75 million-year-old Judith River Formation at Brooks), the story of Weet uses animals from both. One of the best places in our world to see dinosaurs is at the Royal Tyrrell Museum of Paleontology in Drumheller.

Weet's world also contains animals whose fossils have only been found in other parts of our world. Since only a tiny fraction of one percent of living animals become fossils, it is not too wild to assume that something similar to these creatures lived in Southern Alberta and that their bones have just never been found. Here are notes on some of the animals that Weet knew.

SICKLECLAW: Weet's name for velociraptor. These are some of the most beautiful and deadly of all the dinosaurs. They are known from finds in North America and China and ranged in size from five or six feet long to well over 10 feet. They were very like birds and may even have evolved from a flying ancestor such as archaeopteryx. They attacked their larger prey by jumping on it, holding on with their front claws and slashing at it with the sickle-shaped claws on their hind feet. Hardly surprising that they were the subjects of Eric nightmares. No-one knows what colour any of the dinosaurs were, so black and yellow feathers are my choice.

PTERANODON: The pteranodon was a pterosaur. Fragments of pterosaur bones have been found in Southern Alberta. As Eric says, they are not dinosaurs, but lived at the same time. The largest pterosaur, quetzalcoatlus, had a wing span of almost 40 feet. It must have been impressive to see one flapping across the Cretaceous sky.

MARATS: Weet's general name for the small, mouse-like mammals that lived at the same time as the dinosaurs. They probably lived in burrows, only came out at night and never grew larger than a few inches long. They were not very impressive compared to the dinosaurs, yet, you and I are descended from them.

OVIS: Archaeopteryx flew over the lagoons of Europe well before Weet's time. But, perhaps similar flying dinosaurs lived in Weet's world, hunting small prey and gorging on the leavings of the larger predators.

ANKYLOSAUR: If you couldn't outrun a tyranno-saurus, you had to make yourself unappetizing in other ways. The ankylosaurs were armour-plated and probably dropped to the ground when attacked. Thus, the enemy could only break its teeth on the hard armour. The spikes sticking out from the ankylosaur's sides would have prevented a tyranosaurus flipping the animal over to get at its soft belly. If all else failed, the club-like tail could deliver a blow which would seriously injure any predator in search of lunch.

MAIASAURA: A maiasaura nesting site similar to the one where Weet gets his egg has been found and excavated in Montana. It appears that maiasaura lived in herds, cared for its hatchlings and returned to the same site year after year. Maiasaura means "good mother lizard."

EGG-STEALER: These, and the animals seen during the journey to Weet's home, are troodontids. Like velociraptor they were very birdlike. They also had a sickleclaw, although a smaller one. They were smaller than velociraptor and may have hunted marats and small dinosaurs. They were very agile and this may have allowed them to steal the occasional lunch of eggs during the shovelbill nesting season.

SHOVELBILLS: Weet's name for the hadrosaurs or duckbilled dinosaurs. These animals (which included maiasaura, parasaurolophus and lambeosaurus) were very common in the Late Cretaceous. They had a variety of crests on top of their heads which contained air tubes. These were probably used to make a range of calls to warn of danger or to attract a mate. Some reconstructions show them with flaps of skin attached to the crests. These may have been brightly coloured so that the animals could recognise each other.

CRESTNECKS: Weet's name for the ceratopsians. These included triceratops and pachyrhinosaurus and were also very common in the Late Cretaceous. They lived in herds, some of which have been found in graveyards where hundreds of the animals died trying to cross a flooded river.

ROARER: Weet's name for Tyrannosaurus rex. It was much rarer than the crestnecks and shovelbills which it hunted. (In Africa, lions are much rarer than the antelope they hunt.) If you want an idea of what Tyrannosaurus rex was like, imagine a chicken the size of a house with teeth longer than your hand.

SINOR: Weet's pet is based on the dinosaur sinornithoides. A complete skeleton of this animal was recently found in the Gobi Desert in China. Maybe it lived in Alberta too.

WEET: No remains of Weet have ever been found. In fact, he is based on the product of the imagination of Canadian paleontologist Dale Russell. If the dinosaurs had not died out, what would they have evolved into? Possibly intelligent creatures much like us. All I am saying is that this evolution happened before they died out.

HOMS: They are similar creatures to Weet. The only difference is that they are trying to adapt to the changes in their world in a different way.

About the Author

John Wilson grew up on the Island of Skye and in Paisley, Scotland, but since 1978 has made his home in Canada. His university studies earned him a degree in geology which took him initially to Zimbabwe, Africa and eventually to the oil fields of Alberta. Since 1986, when John took a year off to travel around the world, he has been a full-time writer, mining his experiences for arts and travel columns, photo essays, scientific articles, poetry and stories for children. He currently lives in Lantzville on beautiful Vancouver Island with his wife, three delightful children and a dog.